SOFT APOCALYPSES

by

Lucy A. Snyder

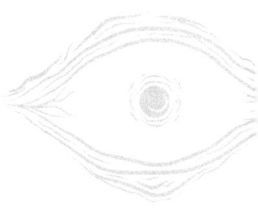

SOFT APOCALYPSES © 2014
by Lucy A. Snyder

Published by Raw Dog Screaming
Bowie, MD

First Edition

Cover Image: Bradley Sharp
Book Design: Jeremy Zerfoss

Printed in the United States of America

ISBN: 978-1-935738-62-6

Library of Congress Control Number: 2014935955

Contents

Magdala Amygdala

I was bound, though I have not bound.
I was not recognized. But I have recognized
that the All is being dissolved,
both the earthly and the heavenly.
—*The Gospel of Mary Magdalene*

"So how are you feeling?" Dr. Shapiro's pencil hovers over the CDC risk evaluation form clamped to her clipboard.

"Pretty good." When I talk, I make sure my tongue stays tucked out of sight. I smile at her in a way that I hope looks friendly, and not like I'm baring my teeth. The exam-room mirror reflects the back of the good doctor's head. Part of me wishes the silvered glass were angled so I could check my expression; the rest of me is relieved that I can't see myself.

Nothing existed before this. The present and recent past keep blurring together in my mind, but I've learned to take a moment before I reply to questions, speak a little more slowly to give myself the chance to sort things out before I utter something that might sound abnormal. My waking world seems to have been taken apart and put back together so that everything is just slightly off, the geometries of reality deranged.

Most of my memories before the virus are as insubstantial as dreams; the strongest of them feel like borrowed clothing. The sweet snap of peas fresh from my garden. The thud of the bass from the huge speakers, and the crush of hot perfumed bodies against mine at the club. The pleasant twin burns of the sun on my shoulders and the exertion in my legs as I pedal my bike up the mountainside.

The life I had in those memories is gone forever. I don't know why this is happening to humanity. To me. I'd like to think there's some greater purpose, some meaning in all this, but God help me, I just can't see it.

"So is the new job going well? Are you able to sleep?" My doctor shines a penlight in my eyes and nostrils and marks off a couple of boxes. Thankfully, she doesn't ask to see my tongue. It's the same set of questions every week; I'd have to be pretty far gone to answer badly and get myself quarantined. The endless doctor-visits wear down other Type Threes, but I hang onto the belief that someday there might be actual help for me here.

I nod. "It's fine. I have blackout curtains; sleep's not a problem. They seem pretty happy with my work."

My new supervisor is a friendly guy, but he always has an excuse for why he can't meet with me in person, preferring to call me on his cell phone for our weekly chats. I used to bounce from building to building, repairing computers, spending equal amounts of time swapping gossip and hardware. After I got out of the hospital, I went on the graveyard shift in the company's cold network operations center. These nights, I'm mostly raising processes from the dead, watching endless scrolling green text on cryptic black screens. I'm pretty sure the company discreetly advised my quiet coworkers to carry Tasers and mace, just in case.

"Do you feel that you're able to see your old friends and family often enough?" Dr. Shapiro asks.

"Sure," I lie. "We meet online for games and we talk in Vent. It's fun."

For the sake of his own health, my boyfriend took a job and apartment in another state; we speak less and less on the phone. What is there to say to him now? We can't even chat about anything as simple as food or wine; I must subsist on bananas, rice, apple juice, and my meager allotment of six Bovellum capsules per day. The law says I can't go to crowded places like theaters and concerts. I only glimpse the sun when I'm hurrying from the shelter of my car's darkly tinted windows to monthly eight a.m. appointments with my court-ordered physician.

So I'm striding up the street to Dr. Shapiro's office, my head down, squinting behind sunglasses, when suddenly I hear a man in the park across the street shouting violent nonsense. Or he used to be a man, anyhow; he's wearing construction boots, ragged Carhartt's work overalls and a dirty grey T-shirt, all freshly spattered with the blood of the woman whose head he is enthusiastically cracking open against the curb. He howls at the sky, and I can see he's missing some teeth. Probably whatever he did for a living didn't pay him enough to see a dentist. But his skin looks flush and smooth, so much healthier than mine, and for a moment I envy him.

He stops howling and meets my shadowed stare, breaking into a gory, gap-toothed smile. The kind of grin you give an old, dear friend. I've never laid eyes on this wreck before, and the woman beneath him is beyond anyone's help. They both are. I don't want to be outed, not here, not like this, so I pretend I don't even see him and stride on.

A few seconds later, I hear the spat of rifle fire and the thud of a meaty body hitting the pavement, and I know that the SWAT team just took out Ragged Carhartts. They're never far away, not in this part of town. And once they've taken out one Type Three, they don't need much excuse to kill another, even if you're just trying to see your doctor like a good citizen.

"Oh, God," a lady says. She and another fortyish woman are standing in the doorway of an art gallery, staring horrified at the scene behind me. They're both wearing batik dresses and lots of handmade jewelry. "That's the third one this month."

"If this keeps up, we'll have to close." The other woman shakes her head, looking grey-faced. "Nobody will want to come here. The whole downtown will die. Not just us. The theaters, the museums, churches—everything."

"I heard something on NPR about a new kind of gel to keep the virus from spreading," the first woman replies, sounding hopeful.

I keep moving. Her voice fades away. People still talk about contagion control as if it matters, as if masks and sanitizers and prayers can stop the future.

The truth is, unless you've been living in some isolated Tibetan monastery, you've already been exposed to Polymorphic Viral Gastroencephalitis. Maybe it gave you a bit of a headache and some nausea, but after a few days' bed rest you were going out for Thai again. Congratulations! You're Type One and you probably don't even know it.

But maybe the headache turned into the worst you've ever had, and you started vomiting up blood and then your stomach lining, and when you came out of the hospital you'd lost the ability to digest most foods and to make certain proteins. And in the absence of those proteins, your body has trouble growing and healing. The enzymes your DNA uses to repair itself don't work very well anymore.

Sunlight is no longer your friend. Neither are x-rays. Even if you quit smoking and keep yourself covered up like a virgin in the Rub' Al Khali, your skin cracks and your body sprouts tumors. Your brain begins to degenerate; you start talking to yourself in second person. Sooner or later, you develop lesions on your frontal lobe and hippocampus that cause a variety of behaviors which will lead to your friendly neighborhood SWAT team putting a .308 bullet through your skull. That means you're a Type Two, or maybe a Type Three, like me.

If you're Type Four, we aren't having this conversation. Unless you're a ghost. You aren't a ghost, are you? I don't think I believe in them. But if you were a Type Four, your whole GI tract got stripped. I hope you were lucky and had a massive brain bleed right when it got really bad, and you never woke up.

I'm pretty sure I woke up.

"Do you find yourself having any unwanted thoughts or violent fantasies?" Dr. Shapiro asks.

"Of course not." I try to sound mildly indignant.

There's one upside, if it can be called that. If you lived past all the pain and vomiting, the symptoms of your chronic disease can be alleviated, if you consume sufficient daily quantities of one of a couple of raw protein sources.

If the best protein source for you is fresh human blood, congratulations, you are a Type Two! Provided you have a fat bank account, or decent health insurance, or are quick with a razor and fast on your feet, you can resume puberty or your athletic career. Watch out for HIV; it's a killer.

If, however, the best source for you comes from sweet, custard-like brains... you are a Type Three. Your situation is much more problematic. And expensive. You better have a wealthy family or truly excellent insurance. Or mob connections. Otherwise, sooner or later, you'll end up trying to crack open someone's skull in public. The only question then is if you'll get that one moment of true gustatory bliss right before you die.

I have excellent health insurance. There's no bliss for me. What I and every other upstanding, gainfully-employed, fully-covered Type Three citizen gets is an allotment of refrigerated capsules containing an unappetizing grey paste. Mostly it's cow brains and antioxidant vitamins with just the barest hint of pureed cadaver white matter. It's enough to keep your skin and brains from ulcerating. It's enough to keep your nose from rotting off. It's enough to help you think clearly enough to function at your average white-collar job.

It is not enough to keep you from constantly wishing you could taste the real thing.

"I was wondering about something," I say, as Dr. Shapiro begins to copy the contents of her survey into the exam room computer.

She stops typing and gives me a wary smile. "Yes, what is it?"

"My medication. I feel okay, you know? But I think I could feel... better. If I could have a little more?" I'm choosing my words as carefully as possible. My tongue feels thick, twitchy.

I can't talk about the cravings I'm feeling. I can't mention wanting more energy, because nobody in charge wants someone like me feeling energetic.

I wonder if there's a sniper watching from behind the mirror on the wall; has he tightened his grip on his rifle? Are gas canisters waiting to blow in the air conditioner vent above me? My skin itches in dread anticipation.

Dr. Shapiro hedges. "Well, I know there's been a shortage of raw materials these days."

I swallow down my impatience and worry. The capsules are ninety-eight percent cow brains, for God's sake. Probably they can squeeze a single human brain for thousands of doses. There are a hundred babies stillborn every day in big city hospitals; some of the mothers have to be altruists. I can't imagine the pharmaceutical companies are running short of anything.

"Could you check, just the same? Could you ask for me?" I sound meek. Pathetic. The opposite of hostile. That's good.

She gives me a pitying look and sighs. The mirror doesn't explode in gunfire. Gas doesn't burst from the vents.

"I'll see what I can do," my doctor says.

I try to believe she'll come through for me.

I go home. I take my capsules with some Mott's apple juice. I rinse my mouth out with peroxide and don't look at my tongue. I rub salve on the places my clothes have rubbed raw, and I climb naked into my bed. Sometime later, the alarm goes off, and I rise, shower, dress, and drive to work in darkness.

My shift is dull-clockwork, until just after grey drizzling dawn, when one of the new tech leads comes in to talk to my coworker George about some of the emergency server protocols. I haven't seen this young man before; he's wearing snug jeans and the sleeves of his black polo shirt are tight over biceps tattooed with angels and devils. His blond hair is cut close over a smooth, high-browed skull. He starts talking about database errors, but he's thinking about a gig he has with his band on Friday night, and it suddenly hits me not just that I know what he's thinking but that I know because I can smell the sweet chemicals shifting inside his brain. The chemicals tell me his name is Devin.

I am filled with Want in the marrow of my bones. I am filled with Need from eyeballs to soles. I excuse myself and hurry out into the mutagenic morning and punch Betty's number into my cell. Soon after we met, she made me promise not to save her details in my phone, just in case anything went wrong.

It's early for her. But she answers on the third ring. Speaking in the casual code we've used since we met online, we agree to meet that evening. It's her turn to host.

I sleep fitfully. When my alarm goes off, I call in sick, shower, dress, and check my phone. Betty's texted a cryptic string of letters and numbers for my directions. And so I drive out to a hotel we've never visited before, drinking Aquafinas the whole way. It's a dark old place, once grand, now crumbling away in a forgotten corner of downtown. I wonder if she's running short of money or if the extra anonymity of the place was crucial to her.

Still, as I get out of my car and double-check my locks in the pouring rain, I can't help but peer out into the oppressive black spaces in the parking lot, trying to figure out if any of the shadows between the other vehicles could be lurking cops or CDC agents. The darkness doesn't move, so I hurry to the front door, head down, hands jammed in my raincoat pockets, my stomach roiling with worry and anticipation. I avoid making eye contact with any of the damp, tired-looking prostitutes smoking outside the hotel's front doors. None of them pay any attention to me.

My phone chimes as Betty texts me the room number. I take the creaking, urine-stinking elevator up four floors. My pace slows as I walk down the stained hallway carpet, and I pause for a moment before I knock on the door of Room 512. What if the watchers tapped Betty's phone? What if she's not here at all? My poised hand quivers as my heart seems to pound out "A trap—a trap—a trap."

I swallow. Knock twice. Step back. A moment later, Betty answers the door, wearing her Audrey Hepburn wig and a black cocktail dress that hangs limply from her skeletal shoulders. It's appalling how much weight she's lost; her eyes have turned entirely black, the whites permanently stained by repeated hemorrhages.

But she smiles at me, and I find myself smiling back, warmed by the first spark of real human feeling I've had in months. I have to believe that we're still human. I *have* to.

"You ready?" Her question creaks like the hinge of a forgotten gate.

"Absolutely." My own voice is the dry fluttering of moth wings.

She locks the door behind me. "I'm sorry this place is such a pit, but the guy at the Holiday Inn started asking all kinds of questions, and this was the best I could do on short notice."

"It's okay." The room isn't as seedy as the lobby and exterior led me to expect it to be, and it's got a couch in addition to the queen-sized bed. Betty has already covered the couch and the carpet in front of it with a green plastic tarpaulin. Her stainless steel spritzer bottle leans against a couch arm.

"Want some wine?" She gestures toward an unopened bottle of Yellow Tail Shiraz on the dresser.

"Thanks, but no... I couldn't drink it right now. Maybe after."

She nods. "There's a really good Italian restaurant around the corner. Kind of a Goodfellas hangout, but everything's homemade. Great garlic bread."

Betty pulls off the wig. Before she got the virus, she could grow her thick chestnut hair clear down to her waist. I've never seen it except in pictures; her bare scalp gleams pale in the yellow light from the chandelier.

The scar circumscribing her skull looks red, inflamed; I wonder if she's been seeing other Type Threes. I quickly tamp down my pang of jealousy. We never agreed to an exclusive arrangement. And maybe she just had to go to the hospital instead; she told me she's got some kind of massive tumor on her pituitary.

She looks so frail. I can't possibly begrudge her what comfort she can get. I should just be grateful that she agrees to see me when I need her.

And, oh sweet Lord, do I need her tonight.

Betty pulls me down to her for a kiss. Her hands are icy, but her lips are warm. She slips her tongue into my mouth, and I can taste sweet cerebrospinal fluid mingled in her saliva. The tumor must have cracked the bony barriers in her skull. Before I have a chance to try to pull away, my own tongue is swelling, toothed pores opening and nipping at her slippery flesh.

She squeaks in pain and we separate.

"Sorry," I try to whisper. But my tongue is continuing to engorge and lengthen, curling back on itself and slithering down my own throat; I can feel the tiny maws rasping against my adenoids.

"It's okay." Her wan smile is smeared with blood. "We better get started."

She kisses the palm of my hand and begins to take my clothes off. I stare up at the tawdry chandelier, watching a fly buzz among the dusty baubles and bulbs. When I'm naked, she slips off her cocktail dress and leads me to the tarp-covered couch.

"Be gentle." She presses a short oyster knife into my hand and sits me down, the plastic crackling beneath me. I nod, barely keeping my lips closed over my shuddering tongue, and spread my legs.

With slow exhalation, Betty settles between my thighs, her back to me. She's a tiny woman, her head barely clearing my chin when we're seated, so this position works best. Her skin is already covered in goose bumps. The anticipation is killing both of us.

I carefully run the tip of the sharp oyster knife through the red scar around her skull; there's relatively little blood as I cut through the tissue. Betty gives a little gasp and grips my knees, her whole body tensed. The bone has only stitched back together in a few places; I use the side-to-side motion she showed me to gently pry the lid of her skull free.

She moans when I expose her brain; it's the most beautiful thing I could hope to see. Her dura mater glistens with a half-inch slick of golden jelly. Brain honey. When I breathe in the smell of her, I feel my blood pressure rise hard and fast.

I set the bowl of skin and bone aside and present the knife to her in my outstretched left hand. With a flick of her wrist, she slits the vein in the crook of my arm and presses her mouth against my bleeding flesh. I wrap my cut arm around her head and pull her tight to my breast.

I open my mouth and let my tongue unwind like an eel into her brainpan. It wriggles there, purple and gnarled, the tiny maw sucking down her golden jelly. It's delicious, better than caviar, better than ice cream, better than anything I've had in my mouth before. Sweet and salty and tangy and perfect.

The jelly gives me flashes of her memories and dreams; she's been with other Type Threes. She's helped them murder people. I don't care. I keep drinking her in, my tongue probing all the corners of her skull and sheathed wrinkles of her brain to get every last gooey drop.

I can control my tongue, but just barely. It's hard to keep it from doing the one thing I'd dearly love, which is to drive it through her membrane deep between her slippery lobes. But that would be the end of her. The end of us. No more, all over, bye bye.

A little of what my body and soul craves is better than nothing at all. Isn't it?

My arm aches, and I'm starting to feel lightheaded on top of the high. We're both running dry. I release her, spritz her brain with saline and carefully put the top of her head back into place. She's full of my blood, and already her scalp is sealing back together. We've done well; we spilled hardly anything on the tarp this time. But my face feels sticky, and I've probably even gotten her in my hair.

She daintily wipes my blood from the corners of her mouth and smiles at me. Her skin is pink and practically glowing, and her boniness seems chic rather than diseased. "Want to go to that Italian place after we get cleaned up?"

"Sure." I'm probably glowing, too. My stomach feels strong enough for pepperoncinis.

I head to the bathroom to wash my face, but when I push open the door—

—I find myself in Dr. Shapiro's office. She's staring down at an MRI scan of somebody's chest. The monochrome bones look strange, distorted.

"There's definitely a mass behind your ribs and spine. It's growing fast, but I can't definitely say it's cancer."

I'm dizzy with terror. How did I get here? What mass? How long have I had a mass?

"What should we do?" I stammer.

She looks up at me with eyes as solidly black as Betty's. "I think we should wait and see."

I back away, turn, push through her office door—

—and I'm back in a rented room. But not the downtown dive with the dusty chandelier. It's a suburban motel someplace. Have I been here before?

The green tarp on the king-sized bed is covered in blood and bits of skull. There's a body wrapped in black trash bags, stuffed between the bed and the writing desk. Did I do that? What have I done?

Oh, God, please make this stop. I have to lean against the wall to keep myself from tumbling backward.

Betty comes out of the bathroom, dressed in a spattered silk negligee. I think it used to be white. There's gore in her wig. Her eyes go wide.

"I told you not to come here!" She grabs me by my arm, surprising me with her strength. In the distance, I can hear sirens. "They'll be here any minute—get away from here, fast as you can!"

She presses a set of rental car keys into my palm, hauls me to the door and pushes me out into the hallway—

—and I'm stepping into the elevator at work.

Handsome blond Devin is in there. A look of surprised fear crosses his face, and I know the very sight of me repels him. His hand goes to his jeans pocket. I see the outline of something that's probably a canister of pepper spray. It's too small to be a Taser.

But then he pauses, smiles at me. "Hey, you going up to that training class?"

I nod mechanically, and try to say "Sure," but my lungs spasm and suddenly I'm doubled over, coughing into my hands. When did simply breathing start hurting this much?

"You okay?" Devin asks.

I try to nod, but there's bright blood on my palms. A long-forgotten Bible verse surfaces in the swamp of my memory: *Behold, I am vile; what shall I answer thee? I will lay mine hand upon my mouth.*

I look up and see my reflection in the chromed elevator walls—my face is gaunt, but my body is grotesquely swollen. I've turned into some kind of hunchback. How long have I had the mass?

Instead of the pepper spray, Devin's pulled his cell phone out. I can smell his mind. He's torn between wanting to run away and wanting to help. "Should I call someone? Should I call 911?"

The elevator is filled with the scent of him. Despite my pain and sickness, the Want returns with a vengeance. Adrenaline rises along with my blood pressure. My tongue is twitching, and something in my back, too. I can feel it tearing my ribs away from my spine. It hurts more than I can remember anything ever hurting. Maybe childbirth would be like this.

Betty. I need Betty. How long has it been since I've seen her? Oh God.

"Call 911," I try to say, but I can't take a breath, can't speak around the tongue writhing backward down my throat.

"What can I do?" Devin touches my shoulder.

And the feel of his hand against my bony flesh is far too much for me to bear.

I rise up under him, grab him by the sides of his head, kissing him. My tongue goes straight down his throat, choking him. He hits me, trying to shake me off, but as strong as he is, my Want is stronger.

When he's unconscious, I let him fall and hit the emergency stop button. The Want has me wrapped tightly in its ardor, burning away all my human qualms. The alarm is an annoyance, and I know I don't have as much time as I want. Still. As I lift his left eyelid, I take a moment to admire his perfect bluebonnet-iris.

And then I plunge my tongue into his eye. The ball squirts off to the side as my organ drills deeper, the tiny mouths rasping through the thin socket bone into his sweet frontal lobe. After the first wash of cerebral fluid I'm into the creamy white meat of him, and—

–Oh, God. This is more beautiful than I imagined.

I'm devouring his will. Devouring his memories. Living him, through and through. His first taste of wine. His first taste of a woman. The first time he stood onstage. He's at the prime of his life, and oh, it's been a wonderful life, and I am memorizing every second of it as I swallow down the contents of his lovely skull.

When he's empty, I rise from his shell and feel my new wings break free from the cage of my back. As I spread them wide in the elevator, I realize I can hear the old gods whispering to me from their thrones in the dark spaces between the stars.

I smile at myself in the distorted chrome walls. Everything is clear to me now. I have been chosen. I have a purpose. Through the virus, the old gods tested me, and deemed me worthy of this holiest of duties. There are others like me; I can hear them gathering in the caves outside the city. Some died, yes, like the ragged man, but my Becoming is almost complete. Nothing as simple as a bullet will stop me then.

The Earth is ripe, human civilization at its peak. I and the other archivists will preserve the memories of the best and brightest as we devour them. We will use the blood of this world to write dark, beautiful poetry across the walls of the universe.

For the first time in my life, I don't need faith. I know what I am supposed to do in every atom in every cell of my body. I will record thousands of souls before my masters allow me to join them in the star-shadows, and I will love every moment of my mission.

I can hear the SWAT team rush into the foyer three stories below. Angry ants. I can hear Betty and the others calling to me from the hollow hills. Smiling, I open the hatch in the top of the elevator and prepare to fly.

However ....
by Gary A. Braunbeck and Lucy A. Snyder

"The great epochs of our lives come when we gain the courage to rebaptize our evil as our best."
–Friedrich Nietzsche, "Fourth Article," *Beyond Good and Evil*

Of the three children it was the youngest, Penny, who was finally able to free herself from the manacles. So emaciated had her limbs become that she easily slipped her left hand through, but her right was still swollen at the base of the index finger and thumb where the bones had been broken. She did not cry out, even though it was obvious to the others that she was in terrible pain. Pausing only long enough to pull in a deep breath, Penny gripped her right wrist and bore down with what little strength remained in her body. Her face turned red from both the agony and the effort, but still she did not cry out.

"Hold on," said Carl, who was older than Penny but not as old as Lewis. "I got an idea. But...."

From his corner of the cramped holding area, Lewis said, "But *what?*"

"It's kinda gross."

"I don't care!" said Penny, tears on her face but nowhere in her voice. "This h-h-h-*hurts!*"

"Do it," said Lewis.

Carl blanched. "But—"

"I already *know* what you're gonna do, okay? And Penny? He's right, it *is* kinda gross."

She pulled in a deep breath. "Will it hurt?"

"It might sting a little."

Penny looked in Lewis' eyes. Lewis—as he always did at times like this, times when the bad things were really, truly, terribly bad—leaned as far toward her as his chains and manacles would allow, smiled at her, and then stuck out his tongue. Penny laughed. On the periphery of his vision—and while he was still making faces at Penny—Lewis watched Carl rise to his feet and walk quietly toward Penny. Carl, though the second oldest of the children, was also the smallest, and the chains binding him to the damp stone walls were heavier.

However, they were also longer. Long enough, in fact, to allow him to get close enough to Penny to touch the back of her head, if he wanted.

Lewis made another face at Penny, who despite her obvious pain started giggling like crazy; he could always make her laugh, even under the worst circumstances. Carl unzipped the front of his pants and peed into his hands, then reached over and poured the warm liquid on Penny's trapped hand. Penny, still giggling, closed her eyes and pulled down once again. Aided now by the lubricant of Carl's urine, her broken hand squeaked through the rusty manacle and she fell back against the wall, whimpering quietly as she cradled her torn, swollen, and bleeding appendage.

Carl was already tearing away part of his shirt to make a bandage. Lewis untied the lace of his left tennis shoe, all the while saying things to Penny like, "That was super brave of you," or "You *so* rock—I wish you were my little sister," or "You're such a great kid and you did *so good*," things to comfort her, to ease her pain, to keep her fear—her terrible, terrible fear—at arm's length.

Working quickly, they dried Penny's hand, wrapped it, and used the shoelace to tie the bandage in place so that the pressure was more or less even. All of this they did in less than one minute; they'd had plenty of practice. Lewis had learned first aid in the Cub Scouts and taught everything he knew to the others; camping and school and his family seemed so long ago, so far away he sometimes wondered if his old life had just been a pleasant dream. His hands knew how to tie a bandage or make a sling, but if he tried to remember the first time he'd done these things, sometimes he was sitting under an oak tree with his scout troop, but sometimes he was sitting here in the basement. The hope that he could get that dream back was all that kept him alive some days. He'd told the other kids time and again that when this day came, they would have to move quickly, no matter how bad all of them felt, or how weak they were because the Cold Ones had taken to starving them for days at a time.

The Cold Ones. Carl had started calling them that because the man was always telling the woman he was going out for "a couple of cold ones". Lewis thought the name fit. What the couple's actual names were—Smith, Jones, Cleaver, Partridge?—none of the children knew, and the longer they were kept down here, the longer they were used as toys, as furniture, as ashtrays, as things to be abused in ways none of them had ever imagined and now would never forget, the longer this went on…the more power the Cold Ones gathered to them. Lewis could feel it. The ice behind their gazes, the frost in their fingertips, the chilly echoes of their voices that seemed to be coming from some dark pit buried deep in the wintry chamber where a human heart should have resided, all these things and more turned them, with every passing minute, into things beyond pain, beyond damage, beyond any Earthbound sensation that might, for a moment, stop them in their tracks.

Penny came over to Lewis and gave him a hug. "I'll be good, you'll see. I'll remember everything you said, Lewis."

"I know you will, Penny." He kissed the top of her head. "But if they come back sooner than we—"

"—I drop everything and just get the box. I know." She pulled away from Lewis, gave Carl a hug, and then limped toward the staircase that led up to the kitchen. She disappeared around the corner and soon they heard the old wooden stairs faintly creaking under her bare feet.

Carl leaned as close to Lewis as he could get and whispered, "What if you heard it wrong? What if the basement door's locked?"

Lewis shook his head. "It didn't make the second click when they closed it this morning. It only clicked once. All she has to do is push it open."

"I can hear you guys," Penny said. It sounded like she was near the top of the stairs. "I ain't gonna touch the doorknob or nothing. I'll push it open."

"That's my girl," said Lewis. He fell silent, listened intently as the she pushed open the door. Both boys stared up as her footsteps moved across the ceiling; she was in the hall heading toward the kitchen.

Lewis' stomach growled. All of them knew where the refrigerator was; they got dragged past the kitchen whenever they were taken to the upstairs living room or bedrooms. Its low hum seemed to taunt him on the nights when his stomach had seemingly transformed into an angry demon inside him. Penny was supposed to get just a few pieces of whatever was there: a couple of slices of American cheese from the fat greasy block in the refrigerator, a couple of pieces of bread if the loaf was already started, a little bologna, a few grapes, maybe an apple if the Cold Ones had a whole bag of them. He'd told her not to touch their fancy gourmet food, that she mustn't take anything obvious, nothing that would be missed. And whatever she did, she mustn't spill anything, or leave any smudges behind to let their captors know she'd escaped from the basement.

"D'ya think she'll do it right?" Carl asked, sounding anxious.

"She's smart; she knows what to do," Lewis replied. "I told her, not one crumb on the floor or the counter. She'll do fine."

"But what if they come back?" Carl was knocking his knees together like he had to pee again.

"They won't," Lewis said, making himself sound more confident than he actually felt. "It's already been more than fifteen minutes." He'd counted it down in his head: *one Mississippi, two Mississippi, three Mississippi ....*

"But they *never* leave together, what if —"

"Carl, *chill*. They used to go out together all the time. But that was before they brought you and Penny down here. If they were gone for more than fifteen minutes, they'd be gone for *hours*. They're going to a secret club or something like that. Meeting people like them and doing *stuff*."

He tried to put enough emphasis on "stuff" to discourage Carl from asking more questions about where the Cold Ones went or what they did. Because Lewis didn't actually know, and told himself he didn't *want* to know, although his imagination got the better of him sometimes. Sometimes the Cold Ones videotaped what they did to him and Carl and Penny; maybe they sold the tapes, and that was how they got money. Or maybe *they* were the ones with the money, and today they were touring another basement in another isolated house. Lewis hoped they were selling the tapes they made, because then maybe the FBI or the sheriff would find one and figure out where they were.

However, if there weren't any tapes for the good guys to find, maybe Penny would find the black box. She sure couldn't use a phone to call for help—the Cold Ones had no phones in the house, they always used their cell phones, they *never* left one of the cells here, and the house was too far out in the country for Penny to try to walk somewhere for help.

Lewis suddenly wasn't sure that she'd follow through on that part of the plan if the couple came home early; even he had to admit that it was confusing to tell her to be really careful about the food, and then turn around and steal something the couple would instantly know was missing. She'd gotten upset at first when he told her to take the box, but calmed down when he told her it was a *magic* box, and if they worked it right, it would help them escape.

He sometimes had to lie to Penny and Carl to keep their spirits up, but the magic in the box was no lie. There'd been many nights when he'd overheard the couple, mostly the man, talking about it, their voices filtering hollowly through the floorboards into the basement. From what Lewis had been able to make out, the box had some tremendous power to grant wishes. Maybe it was sort of like Aladdin's lamp with a genie inside, except it was a puzzle you had to solve instead of just rubbing on it. He'd glimpsed the box himself a couple of times, and Lewis could *feel* the power in it. Usually the Cold Ones kept it locked up in a fancy glass cabinet in the living room, but sometimes, *sometimes*, the man forgot and left it out on the coffee table after he'd been up all night trying to figure out how it worked.

Lewis was good at solving puzzles. At his first day camp one of the counselors brought out an old Rubik's Cube, and he'd been able to solve it way before any of the big kids. By the end of the week, he could solve the thing within two minutes, no matter how messed up it was. And he'd always been able to beat his big brother and his friends at Klax and Tetris. He was dead sure he could do better than their captors.

Penny's footsteps were moving across the ceiling again, and soon he heard the basement door open.

"I got it, guys." Penny padded down the creaky stairs carrying a big white picnic plate piled with odds and ends from the refrigerator and pantry. She had a big, lidded Styrofoam cup tucked under one thin arm, and — Lewis' heart skipped a beat — under the other was the black lacquered puzzle box.

Penny carefully set the plate down on the concrete floor between the boys, then the cup, and then handed the box to Lewis. "It was on the coffee table, like you said. It was on a couple of really old books...they looked important but I couldn't carry them, too."

"That's okay; this is great!" Lewis ran his fingers over the surface of the box, mesmerized. This was the first time he'd been close enough to see that each side of the box was shaped like a face of some sort, but not a human face...or maybe they were faces of things that had once been human but weren't anymore. Oh, whoever had made this was super-smart, some kind of genius, probably. Lewis envied anyone who was that smart, that clever. Just looking at it—even looking at it up close—he couldn't find one seam, one indentation, one pressure point that even *hinted* at how you went about opening it.

Pretend it's like the Rubik's Cube, he told himself. *Pretend that you're doing this on a dare. Pretend that it's something* fun. This was the best way to go, to think of it as a fun game...because, holding it his hands now, feeling as if the six faces were laughing at him, Lewis realized that there was no going back. He *had* to solve it, to open it before the Cold Ones came back. If he didn't, if he was still messing with it when they got home with no genie to help, they would probably kill him — or Penny or Carl — and make him watch.

Fun, he reminded himself. *Think of this as a game, nothing more.*

Carl was already diving into the food, wrapping a cold hot dog in a slice of white bread and stuffing it into his mouth.

"Don't be a piglet; leave some for Lewis," Penny scolded, then turned to the elder boy: "Put that down an' eat something."

"I will, in a minute." His fingers had found a seam in the box, so slight he'd missed it the first time.

"No, *now*," she said, grabbing the box and gently pulling it away from him. "I got pickles just for you."

"Give that back!"

Penny shook her head. "Huh-uh. You gotta be hungry, Lewis, and I don't want you to get sick. I love you."

The rest of the protestations died in Lewis' throat. Penny had never said that to him before, and he realized with something between surprise and *well, duh* that he loved her, as well. Piglet Carl, too.

"I love you, too," he whispered, trying to keep his voice steady.

"You'd better," replied Penny, handing him the pickles and the Styrofoam glass that was filled with milk. "I got the milk from a jug that was half-empty. *No way* they'll notice."

Lewis devoured two pickles, loving everything about the experience: the crunch, the sudden burst of sour sweetness, the juice washing over his tongue and then trickling down his throat. Nothing he'd ever eaten before or would ever eat again could ever taste this good. Except the milk he drank next. And the hot dog after that. And then the bread and cheese.

For a few minutes the three of them sat in silence, eating, sharing the milk, grinning at one another as they chewed their food. After the initial burst of pigging out, they slowed their feasting, not only because they didn't know when they'd eat again and so wanted to savor everything, but also because none of them wanted to eat too fast and make themselves sick. All of them knew how the Cold Ones would make them get rid of each other's sick, and it was not something any of them were in a hurry to repeat.

Penny handed the box back to Lewis and then went over to her section of the wall, sitting down near her chains. "I think I can maybe get my left hand back in," she said, pushing one of the manacles around with her foot, "but there ain't no way this is going back." She held up her bandaged hand.

"If I can get this open," said Lewis, his fingers and thumbs caressing the surface of the box, searching out the seam he'd found earlier, "you won't have to worry about that anymore."

Penny's face brightened. *"Really?"*

"Really. Swear to God."

Carl swallowed the grapes he'd been chewing. "So you weren't lying? That thing really is magic?"

"Yes, it is." *Dear God, please let that be the truth.* "It sure is."

And there it was—the seam. He probed its edges, its surface, the contours of the face in which it was hidden; clockwise, counter-clockwise, side to side, up and down and then—

—*click!*

The sound was so quiet, so soft, so subtle, that none of them should have been able to hear it, but hear it they did, and for a moment all stared in wonder as a section of the box slid out, revealing an interior that was so shiny Lewis could actually see part of his face reflected.

"It's a *music box!*" said Penny, her face suddenly a joyous thing, full of summer afternoons with kites high above.

It took a moment, but then Lewis heard it, as well; a soft tinkling melody like a bird's song at morning.

"Cool," said Carl.

Penny put a finger to her lips. "Shh, Piglet. Leave him alone. You go ahead and work, Lewis. We'll be quiet."

"Thank you."

Lewis lost all track of time after that; for him, the world was the box, its faces, his eight fingers and two thumbs, and the fervent hope that he was still the best puzzle-solver anybody had ever seen.

His fingers danced over the surface of the box, finding more seams that opened to reveal hidden indentations that in turn offered up more clicks. Lewis hunched over the box, possessed by it, enamored of it, his concentration total, his control the strongest it had ever been when confronted with a riddle, brainteaser, or puzzle. Like with the Rubik's Cube in a life that seemed so long ago and no longer part of him, he eventually fell into a rhythm, found his heart beating in time with his breathing while his fingers pressed down in counter-time, on the upbeat. He didn't know how or why but his whole body—his entire *being*, within and without—seemed now to be part of an orchestra, every digit a note, every movement a new instrument joining in the music, every breath a change of key, every *click!* the sound of the conductor's baton tapping against the podium as the next section of the symphony began. Part of him knew the music was coming from the ever-opening box but he would not allow himself to think about that because to do so would invite wonder, and wonder would invite hesitation, and under no circumstances could he hesitate now. The box was offering its secrets up to him, almost as if it were telling him where next to press, to tap, to push, caress and pull.

It's letting *me open it* he thought to himself. *It wants me to succeed.*

His fingers danced a glissando over the six sides once more, and when the final clicks revealed the mirror-like interior of the last six sections, the box came alive in his hands, rose from his palms as if it were a bubble, a leaf in the wind.

And it began to spin. There was no way to tell if it were spinning slow or fast because the interior sections caught the light from the single bulb overhead and turned it into a prism, the colors shooting out and slicing over the surface of the basement walls, the music from within nearly deafening as now the sound of a great pealing bell overpowered all others. Lewis could feel his heart slamming against his ribcage in time with the bell. He looked over and saw that Penny now sat close to Carl, the two of them holding one another, staring at the miraculous thing happening in front of their eyes.

The whirling colors slowed as the dancing box began to spin downward, and with each turn the light in the basement flickered in, then out, until, at the last, everything was cast into a darkness so complete that for an instant Lewis thought he might have just died and discovered that there was no God, after all. Not even a *hint* of a God. Only nothing…except, however, grief and loneliness.

A moment later the single bulb came back on, only now it seemed to glow much brighter than before. Looking around, it seemed to Lewis that the structure of the basement had changed; there were corners where none had been before, and areas once easily seen were now in cavernous shadows. The place even *smelled* different; the overlaying stink that had been their constant companion was gone, replaced by something damp and heavy with rot. Were things like this supposed to happen when you released a genie?

He began to say something to Carl and Penny but the first word came out as a broken whisper and fell to the ground, writhing there for a moment before it crumbled to dust.

Lewis was aware of every aspect of his physical self in so complete a way that he would not have been surprised to hear his very cells talking to one another. Even the house seemed to be breathing. Lewis froze in place, his eyes wide, and that's when the genie that had been hiding in one of the newly shadowed corners began moving into the light.

It is *magic!* Lewis sang within himself, barely able to contain his joy. The box was magic and there was a genie and he knew exactly, *precisely* what his first wish was going to be … but then he pulled in a deep breath and nearly gagged on the damp, heavy stink of rot that assaulted him.

"Who summons us?" said the genie.

Lewis' mouth hung open, lips and tongue dumb meat, made mute by a single word: *us. Who summons* us?

Sounds of movement from other corners, deeper shadows, crept and slithered forward. Lewis looked around once, quickly, and then closed his eyes as he tried to rid his mind of what he'd glimpsed; unable to do that, he willed these sights to break apart, to fragment, to become the disconnected pieces of a picture puzzle that by themselves were still horrible, but so much easier to confront than the whole. This was an old trick he'd taught himself long ago, when the searing ugliness of things he'd seen, things he'd been forced to do, to watch, to imagine, threatened to consume him: take the memory, the image, the lingering sensation and all thoughts connected with it, snap them apart, and scatter them to the wind.

And so he scattered: impressions of things turned inside-out; flayed skin that billowed out like a dress caught in an updraft; fresh, sick-making scars that covered entire bodies; eyes burned closed; noses split down the center and peeled backwards; hooks and nails and staples mangling genitals; shiny black liquid dribbling from torn lips; bowels on the outside stretched into tubes that fed a creature's own filth back into its mouth. Break and scatter, break and scatter.

There.

Facing the first genie—which surely wasn't a genie at all—he steeled himself and opened his eyes.

"I asked a question, boy," said the creature. "Who summons the Order of the Gash?"

"I did," Lewis managed to get out, finally. He shot a quick glance toward Carl and Penny; the two were now wrapped tightly in one another's arms, faces buried in each other's shoulders as they shuddered and whimpered.

Good, he thought. *Stay that way. Don't move, don't speak, and keep your eyes closed.*

The creature moved farther into the light. "And what do you want of us, boy?"

25

"*Boy…*" said another creature somewhere behind Lewis, its voice a mockery, clogged with something thick roiling from a throat equal parts metal and muscle.

The creature that had spoken first stopped moving, looked at Lewis, and then turned its jaundiced eyes toward Carl and Penny. "Oh," it said. And smiled. Its mouth was filled with too many small yellow, jagged teeth, all of them shaped like tiny backward hooks. "The sweet, tender flesh of *children*."

"*Children…*"

"*Such a treat…*"

"*Baby-meat…*"

Hook-Mouth held up one of its hands, silencing the others. "You summoned us, boy. What do you want?"

Lewis looked once more at Penny and Carl. This had been a terrible, horrible mistake, he knew that now, but maybe he could still save them.

"I called you," he said to Hook-Mouth. "They had nothing to do with this."

"Answer me. What do you want of us?"

"Help us get out of here."

Hook-Mouth burst out laughing. "*Help* you? Boy, you have no idea what you've done." It began moving closer and closer to Lewis as it spoke. "We help no one but the Order of the Gash. We are not in the business of saving bodies or souls. We are more interested in *feeding* on them. Slowly, with a dark delight you cannot even begin to imagine."

"Then take *me*. Help them get out of here safe, and take me."

"You don't understand, boy. There is no bargaining here, no deals to be made, no compromises to be reached. *All* of you are coming with us. And knowing as I do how much grief you will feel over the fates of your friends—because their fates *will* be your fault—will only make consuming you more enchanting, and the taste of your suffering even more delectable."

It was so close now that Lewis could feel its diseased breath on his face.

"Ah," said hook-Mouth. "Behold, my brethren—the tears of defeat."

"*Defeat…*"

"*Sweet…*"

"*Baby meat…*"

Hook-Mouth lifted a hand, reaching for Lewis' throat. "You and your friends are going to know such glorious agony, boy. The things we have in store for you are such excruciating pleasures that a useless pile of walking meat like you can never *begin* to—" As soon as Hook-Mouth's hand gripped Lewis' neck, the creature froze.

Lewis felt as if the live end of a power cable had just been jammed into the top of his skull. Everything went white and became anguish—but why should this be any different than the life he and the others had been forced to live for…however long it had been?

Hook-Mouth released Lewis and he slammed back into the wall, then sank to the floor. Carl and Penny gripped each other even more tightly as their shuddering and whimpering intensified.

Hook-Mouth seemed to have lost its balance. It stepped back, its legs—or, rather, the things that had once been legs—shaking. When it pulled in its next breath, it was a ragged, stunned sound. It looked past Lewis to its companions in the shadows and began shouting in a language Lewis had never heard before, but he didn't need to understand it to know the intention behind the words; the inflections were more than enough.

Hook-Mouth was angry, yes, but more than that, it was shaken and confused. After screaming for a few seconds more, it closed its mouth and eyes, regaining its composure.

Lewis struggled back to his feet, making a terrible decision. "Do whatever you need to do. Just … do it fast."

Hook-Mouth, still a bit dazed-looking, shook its head. "We've always known humans like you existed, but I never imagined that we'd…"

It closed its eyes again, for just a moment, and slowly shook its head.

"No," it said, nailing Lewis to the wall with its sickening yellow gaze. "Here you were, and here you'll stay." It moved quickly, placing its hands on Carl's and Penny's heads. The children shrieked and Hook-Mouth laughed—but this time it was not a laugh of mockery, no; this was the sound of a terminal cancer patient laughing at a tumor joke.

"We will go now," it said, and began turning to walk away.

"You can't just leave us here!" screamed Lewis, regretting the words as soon as they were out of his mouth.

Hook-Mouth whirled back to face him. "Oh, yes we can, boy, and that is precisely what we are going to do."

"Why?"

"Because there is nothing we can do to you that hasn't already been done, or that you haven't already imagined! You have *nothing* to offer us. You have wasted our time."

"But—"

"Enough!" Hook-Mouth stared at Lewis for a moment. "I do have to thank you, though, boy. For a moment there, as I shared your pain and your thoughts

and memories, I nearly … envied your remaining here. That will disturb me for a long time to come. It may even pain me. Oh, how I hope it does just that."

"Then if you really want to thank me, get us out of here!" Lewis was only vaguely aware of hearing the back door open upstairs, followed by the sounds of the Cold Ones stomping back inside.

"If you want to thank me, then get us—"

Hook-Mouth only grinned and shook its head once again. "You have nothing to offer us, nothing we want, nothing with which to bargain."

From upstairs there came a loud crash, followed by more stomping, and then a male voice screaming, "If you hadn't gunned the goddamn engine, she wouldn't've run away from me like that! I almost *had her*, you stupid fuckin' cow! She was a pretty little thing, too!"

Hook-Mouth, seemingly intrigued, looked up at the ceiling, listening, following the stomping and sounds of fists hitting flesh with his eyes.

"The box!" shouted the woman. *"Where's the fuckin' box?"*

Lewis bent down and picked up the black box, staring at Hook-Mouth.

Upstairs, the Cold Ones continued to snarl accusations and strike one another.

Lewis held up the box, and began to push the pieces back into place. "Well, if we don't have anything you want…."

"*You* don't," said Hook-Mouth, gazing at the ceiling.

And then, looking at Lewis and grinning broadly: *"However…."*

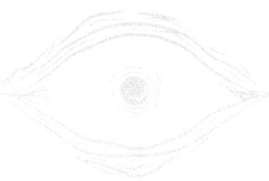

Spare the Rod

Jake Blevins was finishing his third mug of Budweiser when he finally confessed to his brother: "I'm gettin' real worried about Ricky. I found him in his ma's makeup case the other day. He painted his toes pink. *Pink*."

Sam set down his own mug and gave Jake a concerned frown. "Did you discipline him proper?"

"I ... I did my best." He took another swig of brew to quench his suddenly-dry mouth. His hand shook, he hoped not so badly that Sam could see. "I yelled at him and slapped the box outta his hands—broke the hinge, I got an earful about that later from his ma—and made him take the paint off with turpentine in the garage."

"But did you spank him?"

The question made bile and beer rise in Jake's throat. For a moment he thought he might puke right there on the cigarette-burned Formica table. Maybe talking to Sam about this was a bad idea. But who else did he have to go to besides his brother? He knew what his father would say if the old man were still alive. He knew what the parish priest would say; hell, Father Walton would probably offer to punish the boy himself.

His wife had made it clear she didn't approve of spankings, ever, but she was just a woman. It wasn't her place to boss him, and it wasn't his place to listen to her. He was the *paterfamilias*, and discipline was his responsibility.

"I yelled at him for a long time, and he seemed plenty scared when I was done," Jake replied.

Sam shook his head, his frown deepening into a scowl. "That ain't good enough."

"I don't think he'll do it again—"

"Are you tryin' to raise up a God-damned faggot?" Sam slammed down his mug, but the bar jukebox was too loud for anyone to pay any attention. He

29

looked horrified and furious. "You want your boy's soul to burn in everlastin' hell because you didn't have the stomach for good discipline?"

Jake felt as though he'd been slapped in the face. "No, of course I don't."

"You know as well as I do that a boy who plays around with makeup is well on the road to faggotry. You gotta nip that in the bud! Today it's painted toes, tomorrow he'll be into his mother's unmentionables dressin' up like a queer ... you gotta beat some man into him. Spare the rod and spoil the child."

"But he's only seven."

"Seven?" Sam snorted. "That's plenty old enough for a spanking. I was eight when Pa gave me my first. My boys were six. And you was seven, though I reckon you don't remember too much 'bout that."

For just a moment, Jake felt as though he were back in his old room at the farmhouse, his father grabbing him by the back of his neck and throwing him down on the bed. It was all happening because Jake had cried and refused to help his father and uncles slaughter the calves. He'd been taking care of one calf since she was born, and he loved her like he loved his puppy Rufus. He couldn't bear to put the knife to her throat.

"If you ain't willin' to do man's work, that makes you a goddamn *girl*, and I ain't raisin' no girls in this house," his father had thundered as he pulled Jake's jeans and underwear down around his ankles. "You wanna be a girl, boy? I'll show you what's it's like to be a girl!"

His own blood was a freight train in Jake's ears, the remembered agony and terror and his shame at not being able to take his punishment like a man almost overwhelming, and he wished for the ten thousandth time since he was seven that the Earth would open up and swallow him and leave no trace behind.

"Pa spanked the devil out of you." Sam paused to drain his own mug in a single gulp. "I reckon Ma was sure you'd bleed to death, and she finally got Uncle Eustace to take you to the county hospital. Sheriff Andy came by and gave Pa a talking-to. Almost hauled him in. You recollect any of that?"

Jake shook his head numbly. Bits and pieces of the spanking and his hospital stay circled like sharks through his nightmares, but he couldn't be sure what was a real memory and what was just a figment of his imagination.

Sam laughed with a good-times humor that didn't match the darkness in his eyes and slapped Jake on the shoulder. "Don't matter if you remember it ... the important thing is you butched right up and flew straight! Wasn't a boy in the whole state more eager to help with the slaughters than you! Pa didn't have to spank you but a few times after that to keep you in line, did he?"

"Three," Jake replied.

He seldom dared to remember his Pa's fourth attempt. He was fifteen. Sam was off in the Army by then. Jake had crashed the tractor when he hit an unseen sinkhole; after he got himself out from under the hulk he'd run to the barn to escape the old man's wrath. When his Pa came after him, he grabbed a rusty scythe ... and he didn't remember much more after that but coming to and seeing the blood and entrails dark against the straw and the whitewashed walls. His Ma found him out there, and she held him for a while and helped him clean everything up. Nobody ever found the place by the creek where they planted his Pa.

Jake still blacked out sometimes, and came awake in his car or standing in an alley someplace with blood on his clothes and hands. He never went looking to see where it had come from. Once he found a severed finger in his pocket. He threw away all his knives after that. Still, sometimes he'd find blood under his fingernails or in the treads of his work boots and have no idea what had happened.

"He spanked me three times in my whole life," Jake said.

"Three times, and you turned out just fine!" Sam gave him another shoulder-slap.

Then he leaned forward across the baskets of chewed-up gristle and discarded chicken bones and spoke to Jake more softly: "Look, I know you don't want to hurt your boy, but pain is good for a young man. It builds character. Pa spanked me twice, and yeah, I hated him for it.

"But he was preparin' me for the world, Jake. If he hadn't given me proper discipline, I'd have never survived what the Serbs did to me when they captured my squad. The pain Pa put me through was a gift that kept me strong, kept my mind clear, and when I had my chance I got free and killed every last one of those sonsabitches with my bare hands. And then me and my boys went down to the nearest village and gave 'em all a taste of good ol' American payback. I kept some baby teeth as souvenirs; I knew Sarge would have confiscated anything else once we were back on base."

Sam paused, looking as serious as Jake had ever seen him. "Do right by your son, brother. Don't let him grow up to be some God-forsaken faggot. Make sure he grows up strong like us."

Jake poured the rest of their pitcher into his mug. Maybe Sam's advice was solid. Maybe spankings were like vitamins: too much or too little made you sick and weak. Maybe if he just spanked his son once, and didn't do it so hard or for so long that the boy passed out and couldn't remember it clearly afterward, he'd never have to do it again.

"Okay," Jake said. "You're right."

"I'm glad you're seein' things more clearly." Sam nodded grimly and raised his mug in a salute. "Sometimes it's hard to spank a boy the first time, and there ain't no shame in that; I got some little blue pills that'll help if you think ya need 'em. And make sure you use some lard. Not too much, or it won't hurt enough."

"I will," Jake promised. "I will."

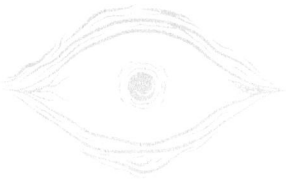

Miz Ruthie Pays Her Respects

Andrew Dockholm straightened his navy blue JROTC uniform and stepped through the automatic doors leading to the Hillsonville Regional Airport's baggage claim area. He spotted a tall, silver-haired woman in an ankle-length black dress by the lone conveyor belt. She clutched a leather purse and a bouquet of yellow roses and white lilies in her left hand, and was leaning over to try to catch a small blue suitcase with her right. The woman looked just like her pictures on Facebook, except for the black dress; she was mostly dressed in flowery hippie clothes in those.

"Let me get that for you, Miz Ruthie!" Andrew shouldered his way through the sparse crowd so he could get to the light suitcase before his cousin did.

"Oh! Andrew. Hello there. I could've gotten that, but thank you." Ruthie blinked at him, looking surprised, then glanced past him, her expression darkening. "Is your mother or your father with you?"

"No ma'am. I got my regular driver's license last week, so I just came on out here in my truck after drill practice." Andrew beamed at her.

"Do your folks know you're picking me up?" She looked a bit worried, and maybe a touch suspicious.

"Not exactly, ma'am...I got the feeling they don't cotton to you much. Don't know why 'cuz you seem like a real nice lady in your emails, and you always give me good loot in Mafia Wars, and we're family, right?"

Andrew's folks had never made the cause of their disapproval clear, although once when his pa had too much Wild Turkey and had gone on a drunken rant he'd called Miz Ruthie "That Frisco witch." His pa never had much compunction about calling women the b-word, so the witch thing had made Andrew curious, but later his pa denied having said it and went silent as a lowcountry clam about their cousin. Miz Ruthie had posted stuff supporting Obama on Facebook, but Andrew supposed he could turn the other cheek on that because women usually had stupid ideas about politics. And she'd posted stuff about doing Tarot readings, which his grandpa preached was Satanic, but Andrew had seen a Tarot deck at a gaming store once and as far as he could tell it was just paper and ink like a regular playing card deck. He didn't see what was so bad about it besides that one devil card. It wasn't like she was a Muslim or something.

"It's only right you want to pay your respects to my grandpa," Andrew continued. "The whole county came out for his funeral last weekend. It wouldn't be right to make a lady like you take a taxi."

After all, Miz Ruthie had to be at least fifty, practically as old as his own grandma, but he knew better than to tell her that. Old ladies didn't like you pointing out that they were old. Andrew figured he wouldn't be much of a man if he didn't step up and offer to take his cousin out to the family graveyard. Besides, he liked showing off his new truck, a Dodge Ram with a hemi V8 engine. He'd worked three solid years of weekends and summers down at the sawmill to save up for it—had to get his pa to lie about his age to the owner at first—but at fourteen Andrew had been as big and strong as any sixteen-year-old. And besides, like his pa and grandpa had always said, all those labor laws were just dumb government meddling.

Ruthie still looked worried. "Well, I wouldn't want you to get in any trouble...."

"I ain't gonna get in no trouble! I stay out late all the time, and my pa don't care as long as I do my chores."

"What about your mama?"

Andrew blinked at her. "What about her? She don't wear the pants."

Despite Miz Ruthie's gentle protestations, Andrew insisted on carrying her suitcase out to his truck. He took a moment to pop the hood to show her the engine, clean and pretty as a prom queen's pussy, and tell her how fast it went up the road to Table Rock Mountain. And then they were off, speeding down the highway toward the turnoff to the old stone church where all their kin were buried, including Andrew's grandpa, the Reverend Robert M. Dockholm, who'd presided over New Bedrock Baptist Church for over thirty years.

"So are you going into Air Force ROTC in college?" Miz Ruthie asked, gesturing toward his uniform.

"No ma'am, I'm gonna be an Army Ranger. I already got it all worked out with the recruiter. I'm only in Air Force JROTC 'cuz that's all they have at my high school."

"What about college?" she asked.

"College? I already got a job, I don't need no college."

"Ah."

Andrew pulled his truck into the gravel parking lot in front of the old stone church; since it didn't have electricity or indoor plumbing, the congregation only used the 180-year-old building for weddings and funerals in good weather. The lights of the New Bedrock Baptist Church were visible on the hill beyond. The evening sky was a solid ceiling of gray clouds, and the piney air hung moist and heavy. Thunder rolled somewhere in the distance.

"Well, I'll do my best to keep this quick so you don't have to wait out here too long," Miz Ruthie said, glancing out the window at the ominous sky.

"Oh, I'm gonna go into the cemetery with you."

Miz Ruthie bit her lip. "It would probably be better if you just stayed here."

"No ma'am! It's gettin' dark out there, and what if you was to trip on a root, or twist your ankle in a gopher hole? I'd be failin' my duty if didn't escort you proper."

"Okay." She frowned; clearly she was turning something over in her mind. "But I need to pay my respects in my own way, and I want you to promise you won't interfere with me."

"Sure, I promise." He drew an X over his heart with his finger. "Soldier's honor."

"All right then." She opened her door and stepped out onto the gravel with her funeral bouquet, then gave him a sharp look. "You better remember your promise; if you don't like something, don't look."

Andrew squinted at her, wondering what she meant, and followed close behind as she made her way up the path into the graveyard. The first part of the cemetery was the oldest, some graves dating to the early 1800s. They walked among the mottled, decaying marble stones, some so worn that he could barely make out that there had ever been inscriptions on them. The ground was a patchwork of velvety dark moss, gravel-embedded soil, and short green grass.

Andrew ran his hands over the tops of the headstones as he walked, the worn stone rough and gritty. Some of these people were born before the nation had its independence. All had died before it was torn by the War Between the States. He felt a surge of pride; he and his JROTC squad had spent several weeks after school cleaning up the cemetery, clearing brush and weeds away from the old markers and headstones and crypts. His grandpa had told him they'd done a right fine job.

Old stones gave way to newer markers and crypts. The inscriptions became recognizable, and so were the family names. Hillson. Harris. Keller. Smith.

Calhoun. Dockholm. Andrew watched as Miz Ruthie went to her mother's grave, pulled three lilies from the bouquet, and laid them on her headstone.

But then, instead of heading to the Reverend Dockholm's freshly-mounded grave near the edge of the trees, Miz Ruthie went to a headstone tucked back amongst the graves of townsfolk who weren't their kin, except maybe by marriage. She knelt at the forgotten grave, laid the bouquet down, and spent several minutes kneeling there with her head bowed.

Andrew tried to stand at easy attention while she paid her respects to whoever it was, but just as he was starting to feel really antsy she got up and headed toward his grandfather's resting place, her hands empty. Shouldn't she have some flowers to pay proper respects? Frowning, he followed her over to the grave.

She held up her hand. "Remember, you promised: no interfering."

Miz Ruthie pulled a travel pack of Kleenex out of the pocket of her long black dress—

That's good, she's going to have a big ol' cry over him like my momma did, Andrew thought.

—which she shoved down the front of her dress, apparently into her cleavage. And then she unzipped the dress from neck to hem. Andrew felt his face flush crimson as she shrugged out of the dowdy old-lady garment, revealing that she was wearing a short stoplight-red cocktail dress and gartered fishnet stockings beneath. Miz Ruthie had a really nice ass, and Andrew felt his blush deepen as he realized he'd gotten a rubbery boner at the sight of her in the clingy satin. She was old enough to be his granny, for sweet Jesus' sake!

Miz Ruthie folded the black overdress and set it on a nearby headstone, then strode to the Reverend's grave and began dancing, sweeping the flowers off his headstone with her lean legs.

"Miz Ruthie, what are you doing?" Andrew was aghast.

"Paying all the respects I owe your grandfather." Her skirt rode up with each Rockette kick, and he saw a sterling silver flask strapped to the outside of her left thigh. "Remember, you promised. Crossed your heart and promised."

Once she'd cleared off the headstone, she stood facing it with her legs on either side of the grave, did a half-squat and hiked her skirt up to her hips. She wasn't wearing any underwear. Andrew watched, horrified and hard, as she made a V with her fingers and pulled up on her pussy, and suddenly she was peeing in a strong arc right on the headstone, urine spilling down the words "In Loving Memory of the Reverend Robert M. Dockholm."

Lucy A. Snyder

Andrew was rooted to the spot, unable to move or speak in his shock. A thousand thoughts crowded in his head, which was about 999 more than usually occupied the space. She was defiling his grandfather's grave! Vandalizing it! And she. Could. Pee. Standing. Up! Andrew had never heard of women doing such a thing. Was she one of those freaky chicks with a dick? He couldn't see anything like a penis, not even a little Cheeto-looking one like that kid in gym class had. No wonder his pa thought she was a witch!

Ruthie's pee stream faltered, stopped, and she swiveled around and did a deeper squat so that her ass was nearly touching the soil. And she began to shit, the poop coming out of her in a long, smooth coil, mounding in perfect circles like soft-serve on the grave. As she grimaced in concentration, gritting her teeth, grinding her hips in circles to squeeze out the poop *just so*, he began to suspect she'd been practicing. And also probably eating a whole lot of prunes on the plane ride from California.

Andrew's vision was starting to darken at the edges, his legs shaking beneath him, so he went with it and fell to his knees, shutting his eyes against his cousin's abominations and loudly repeating every prayer and psalm he could remember.

As he spoke, "The Lord is my strength and shield; my heart trusts in Him and I am helped," inside he was praying, *Dear God, strike this wicked witch down with your Almighty wrath, please dear God, oh please, strike her down.*

His hair rose on end, the air going electric, and a heartbeat later there was a sudden crack of lightning in the trees nearby and one of the tall pines shrieked as its trunk was sundered near the roots, and Andrew could hear it falling—

"Andrew, get out of the way!" Miz Ruthie shouted.

He opened his eyes to see the pine tree plummeting straight down toward his head, no time to stand up. He frog-hopped forward, but the tree slammed down on his right leg, pinning him to the mossy ground, the pain a bright blue spark arcing from his ankle right up into his spine.

Miz Ruthie was still in full squat, but was vigorously wiping herself clean with a handful of the Kleenex she'd stashed in her bra; she dropped the crumpled tissues neatly around her poo-swirl, completing the first-glance illusion that it was some kind of ice cream dessert. Then she stood, pulled her flask out of her thigh holster, unscrewed the cap, and poured the liquid inside over her shit sundae. Andrew smelled strong whisky. She stepped aside, pulled a packet of matches out of her bra, and lit up her pile, filling the air with the stench of burning feces.

Miz Ruthie strode over to him and squatted near his head, frowning down at him. He tried not to stare at the dark furry fringe peeking from beneath the hem of her dress.

"Is your leg broken?"

"No, ma'am, I don't think so." His voice was a dry croak. He'd broken his leg when he fell off a pile of logs at the mill once, and aside from the initial pain his leg wasn't hurting nearly as badly as it had back then.

"Did you pray for God to strike me down?" Her sharp blue eyes bored down into his, daring him to tell her a lie.

He tried to shrink back into the tree's branches. "Yes, ma'am. I did. But...but you deserved it for what you done to my grandpa!"

She laughed at him. "Oh, I did, did I? Let me tell you a little something about just desserts, boy. Let me tell you a little something about that dead old bastard over there that you hold in such high regard.

"Dear ol' Uncle Bob there took over the church when I was about your age, still in high school. My best friend in the whole world was a girl named Jenny; she was the finest fiddle player in the whole state, sweet as orange blossom honey, smart. Would have made a hell of a doctor some day. One afternoon, one of her older cousins offered her a ride home from school, only he didn't take her home; he drove out to the old bridge and raped her. She was so wrecked she wouldn't even talk to me about what he'd done to her, but when she realized she was pregnant, she went to Uncle Bob for help. She thought he surely knew *everything*, and would make things right. And Uncle Bob, ever the student of Christ's wisdom and forgiveness, cussed her out for telling lies about her choir-boy cousin and accused her of being a whore. Jenny left the church in tears, went to her room and wrote me a letter, then went out to the woods behind her family's house and killed herself. Her father passed her suicide off as a hunting accident so she could be buried over there in this rusty old cemetery."

Ruthie nodded toward the headstone where she'd left her bouquet, then pointed a shaky finger at his grandfather's grave. "The Reverend Robert M. Dockholm might as well have loaded the shotgun, put it to Jenny's head and pulled the trigger. As far as I'm concerned, he murdered that girl. Bob deserved to be broken like he broke Jenny, deserved a load of buckshot right between his sanctimonious eyes, but instead he got thirty more years of respect as the pillar of the community, thirty years of ill-gotten wealth by spiritually blackmailing all the sick old folks in the county into signing their worldly possessions over to his church. Jenny's cousin at least had the decency to pick a fight in a biker bar and get his head caved in with a tire iron the year after he assaulted her, but that Bible-waving sack of shit over there got to enjoy a nice life and a nice quiet death. And so tonight he got me paying my respects the best way I know how."

Miz Ruthie stood up and put her fists on her hips, glaring down at Andrew. "There's a whole lot more you need to know about this fine little town and the people who live in it, but it's up to you whether you want to open your eyes and get a clue about the world, the *real* world, and get out of that nice warm pile of small-town bullshit you've been wallowing in. And here's clue number one: God isn't your personal hit man. I learned that a long time ago, because believe me, I prayed for Him to take out your grandfather. You pray for anyone else's death ever again, boy, you best be prepared for your own."

She inhaled like a diver preparing for a plunge. "So. You've got two choices here. Your first choice is to close your eyes and start praying again, pretending I'm not really here, and I'll call a cab to take me to the airport and call the VFD to come get this tree off you. You'll never have to hear from me again. Your second choice is you take my hand, I'll help you up, and I'll get dressed and we'll go down the road to the Steak and Shake. I'll buy you a malt and tell you all about the skeletons in the family closet.

"So what's it gonna be, Andrew?"

The boy stared up at her, took his own deep breath, and held out his hand.

The Good Girl

My cell chimed just after I fell asleep. Swearing, I fumbled for it on the nightstand. I was sure I'd set the thing to vibrate. I stared at it blearily, wondering if I should just let it go to voicemail.

Sharonda stirred sleepily beside me. "You gonna get that?"

Polite reflex overrode my better instincts. "Yes."

I punched the answer button and pressed the phone to my ear. "Hello?"

"Praise Jesus, I finally got through to you, girl." My father's voice was faint over the bad connection.

Shock ran down to the soles of my feet. My parents and I hadn't spoken for fifteen years. I'd thought they were out of my life for good.

"Hi ... Dad." The words threatened to stick on my tongue.

In the darkness beside me, Sharonda inhaled in surprise. The bed creaked as she sat up, listening.

I continued, casual, as if this was an everyday conversation: "How's it going?"

"Well, I reckon I have some bad news. It's your sister. She got the cancer. She don't have much time."

"Oh no." It had been two decades since I'd last seen Leanna. I had no idea she'd been back in touch with our folks. The last time we'd talked, she'd made it clear she was done with all of us.

I don't have nothing 'gainst you, Maybelle, she told me at the Greyhound station. *You were always real good to me. But I can't go on livin' if I have to keep rememberin', and you're a reminder.*

"I'm real sorry to hear that." I winced at the sound of my own voice. All those years of trying to fit into Middle America and suddenly my Southern accent was creeping back.

41

"She wanted to see you before the Good Lord takes her," my father said, his voice hollow and echoey. "You reckon you could get down here to pay a visit? She surely would appreciate it. Your ma and me would, too."

"I'll try."

"Praise Jesus. You always were such a good girl."

We said our goodbyes and I ended the call. My heart was thudding and I was sweating like I'd just sprinted around the block.

"That was my father. I have to go to South Carolina."

Sharonda fumbled on the light and just stared at me for a moment. "You're actually going down there?"

"He says my sister's dying. I should see her."

"Oh, Belle. No. I'm so sorry, but ... you couldn't save her then, and you can't save her now."

I hugged my pillow to my chest. "I could have tried harder. Part of me knew what was happening, and I just ... I did nothing."

"You were just a child, honey. What could you do?"

"Something. *Anything.* Shit." I wiped hot tears from my eyes. "If she's there now, that means either she's got no place else to go, and this is a living nightmare for her ... or it means he's genuinely changed and they've reconciled. Either way, I should go see her."

"How did that old bastard get your cell number anyway? It's not enough that you had to spend the last ten years in therapy to get him out of your head?"

I rubbed my temples. "Dr. Boyle said it was important to know that I am better than he is. To know that I can rise above everything that happened. How can I know that if I can't even face him?"

Sharonda was silent for a long moment.

"I know where you're coming from, but I don't think I can go with you," she finally said, twisting the white sheets around her dark fists. "I'd kill him. The moment I saw his face I'd punch what was left of his teeth straight down his throat. I don't care if he's changed. That man deserves to be torn apart by pigs for what he did to you and your sister."

I squeezed her arm to show her I understood and wasn't disappointed. "It's okay. I think I only have enough frequent flier miles to cover my ticket anyway."

Sharonda hugged me tightly. "Do what you need to, baby. But promise me this: don't stay at his house. Anything gets weird down there, you get the hell out, okay?"

"Okay, I promise."

On the plane to Hillsonville, I wondered what I really did owe my family. I knew how things were supposed to work. A good daughter would visit her father. A good woman would go to her sister's deathbed. A good person would forgive and forget. It was so simple to turn the other cheek right up until the day you got a broken jaw.

I stared down at my trembling hands. They'd always reminded me of my father: we both had the same slight bend in the first joints of our ring fingers. I heard his voice every time I cleared my throat. I couldn't burn his winding genes away no matter how much I wished I could.

At least I could console myself that I wasn't the same little girl who'd first thought of committing suicide at the age of 12. I'd gotten out and grown up. I'd done my best to break the cycle. Tied my tubes so no child would ever suffer because of the jagged ways I'd been raised. Even if I was stuck with half his DNA, I wasn't passing it on, and the atoms in my body had cycled in and out at least three times.

I was my own person now. And that had to mean something.

I hailed a yellow cab outside the Hillsonville Regional Airport. The cabbie pulled up to the curb and got out, smiling at me. He was a thin brown kid in a starched white camp shirt and skinny jeans.

"Do you have any luggage besides your backpack, ma'am?" He pushed a pair of designer glasses up his nose.

I shook my head. "I'm only staying a few days."

He eyed my orange pack as he came around to open the back door for me. "That's a weekender model, right? Those are nice. You can fit a whole lot in those with compression packers."

"Sure can." I got into the back of the taxi and he shut the door. "I did a whole week in California once with just this and my laptop bag."

"My name is Alonzo, by the way." He slid into the driver's seat and flipped on the cab's meter. "Where can I take you this afternoon?"

"The Comfort Inn off 178," I replied.

"Oh, that's a good place. You get your room online...?"

Alonzo kept up his friendly, low-key chat all the way to the hotel. He was going to college up in Ohio but was staying with an aunt near the airport that summer to earn some money for the upcoming semester. I liked him; I wished I'd known someone like him when I was in high school. Wished I'd been able to know someone like him. As far as my father was concerned, my only friends could be Jesus and his apostles.

At first, it was simultaneously pleasant and painful to hear Alonzo talk about his family: normal, flawed human beings who wrangled and squabbled but ultimately behaved like people who cared about each other. But the fun of living vicariously through strangers always wears off.

So when I felt my hands start to shake in the way I knew would be hard to stop once they really got going, I gently redirected the conversation back to Alonzo's schooling, and he was more than happy to chatter about that instead.

"... so if it all goes right, I'll have my degree and be able to get my social worker's license soon after."

"And then you'll be pulling down the big bucks, right?" I joked. My legs jittered behind the passenger seat.

"Right." He laughed as he pulled into the parking lot of the Comfort Inn. "But I mean, I don't have kids, so I won't need much money. I feel like if I can help people, I should, right? I saw some bad stuff growing up, but I had it easier than lots of kids. My daddy always said, society's only as strong as the weakest links, so ... I want things to be better for everybody, you know?"

"You're a good guy, Alonzo."

He laughed again. "I try. I don't always make it to church, you know? My aunt gets after me about that."

Alonzo totaled up my taxi ride, and I paid him in cash. He brightened considerably when he saw the tip.

"Hey, thanks. Do you think you'll need a ride anywhere later?" he asked.

"Yes. Could you come back around 6pm?"

Alonzo got me to the gate in front of my father's property just before dusk. My hands trembled the entire ride out, but I did my best to keep him from seeing my fear.

He squinted uncertainly at the rusty chain link gate and the rutted gravel road that seemed to disappear into a gloom of pine trees and kudzu. "You sure this is where you need to be?"

"Very sure." I pulled my wallet out of my back pocket and handed him the cash I owed him for the ride. I tried to do it quickly so he wouldn't see that I was shaking so badly.

But he saw, and he looked at me, concerned, as he took the bills. "Are you *really* sure you want to be here?"

I forced myself to smile. "I'm not planning to stay, so I'll call you when I'm done here, all right?"

"Yes, ma'am. I'll be on duty until midnight."

I got out of the cab, waved to Alonzo, and pushed open the gate. It was in desperate need of oil. Back in the woods to my left I could see a cell phone tower, the kind that was made to look like a pine tree. It had to be just inside the neighbor's property; my father would never let someone build a transmitter on his land. When I was little, I'd heard him rant about demons traveling into people's souls through radio signals. If the local AM country station was a force for Satan, I could scarcely imagine the threat of AT&T.

On second glance, the cell tower looked ... dead. Kudzu, so darkly green it looked nearly black in the fading evening light, had climbed nearly to its top. The suffocating vines had wound their way through the artificial branches. I pulled my phone out of my pocket to check my bars. No service.

I stepped back to flag down Alonzo, but he'd already driven out of sight down the highway. My stomach dropped and I swore softly to myself. Wait. My father called me, so he must still have landline service. It would be fine. I wasn't stranded there in the woods. It would be fine.

I took a deep breath to steady my nerves, and began the quarter-mile hike up the road to the house.

The wretched condition of the front gate made me fear what I'd find at the top of the hill, but the house and yard looked exactly the same as I remembered it: tidy cedar shingles on the roof, fresh-painted sky-blue siding, the broad wrap-around porch, the wide oak stump my father used for splitting pine logs for the stove.

I remembered the rough wood splintering my cheek as my father forced my head down onto the cutting stump, gravel biting into my knees and palms, the Lord's Prayer shuddering from my lips as I begged my father not to kill me for talking to a boy at the convenience store –

I forced myself to look away and stare at the red hummingbird feeder my mother liked to look out on while she cooked meals.

Her silhouette flickered past the kitchen window, head dark against the yellow kitchen light. That's how I mostly remembered her: quiet, in the kitchen, cooking or cleaning, a dutiful Christian wife who only spoke when she was spoken to and deferred to her husband in all matters. She was the fifth of ten kids who grew up in a three-room house in the Smoky Mountains, and I guess my father looked like salvation when he stopped at the diner she'd had to waitress in since she was 14.

Food was the truest love she'd ever known, and every meal she made was a humble feast. We never went hungry except for the occasional week my father's mood swung and he decided God had called on him to starve the Devil out of us.

I could smell ham and biscuits baking in the oven, and my mouth began to water despite the huge chef salad I'd had at the restaurant beside the hotel. I'd resolved to myself that I would be polite in my father's home, but I would not accept any more of his and my mother's hospitality than was necessary. They'd shunned me for fifteen years, and I wouldn't let them treat me like family now. I wouldn't even eat so much as the proverbial six pomegranate seeds there if I could help it.

I went to the front door and knocked.

"Just a minute," I heard my mother call.

Moments later, the door opened. My mother was there dressed in one of her home-stitched gingham dresses and her favorite yellow apron decorated in embroidered blue clematis flowers and curling vines.

"Maybelle, we missed you so much!" Not quite meeting my gaze, she grabbed my hand in hers and pulled me into the house. She didn't try to hug me, but she was never much of a hugger. "Your daddy is in the living room waiting for you."

"Is Leanna here?"

"She's taking a nap. Poor thing gets so tired. I need to get back to dinner—can't let the greens scorch! We'll have a chance to set a spell and catch up after dinner."

And with that, she disappeared into the kitchen again. I stood there in the hallway, breathing in ancient house dust, willing my heart to stop hammering. This was a nice place now. A perfectly nice place.

My father's artwork covered the walls. He made his own frames and cut his own glass to size. He'd started out selling portraits and landscapes at fairs and festivals around the state, and from what I heard he made a good living at it. But by the time I was five, his mind had turned in on itself and after that he only sketched religious figures, mostly Jesus. In the biggest piece above the entryway to the living room, he'd portrayed Christ with a square jaw, fierce eyes and flowing blond hair, as though the Savior was some Viking conqueror. He even had a sword tucked in a studded belt.

My gaze fell on the closed sewing room door. My heart started pounding again. Funny how one old brass knob and plain wooden door could be so thoroughly terrifying.

I was eleven and Leanna was fifteen when our father went from religious eccentricity to predatory insanity. After her birthday, he found a card from a boy in her book bag, and he was furious. He made her take a purity pledge at church, but that wasn't enough. He started going into her bedroom at night to make sure she hadn't been "sinning".

I knew what he was doing to her. I should have comforted her. I should have tried to protect her. I should have gotten the rifle down from the mantel and blown the sick bastard out of his boots. But I didn't do any of that. I pretended I couldn't hear him violate her, couldn't hear her weeping afterward.

Nobody in the house was surprised when her belly started to swell. But I feared the worst. I was scared he'd take her out in the woods and I'd never see her again.

But our father's whole attitude changed. He was ecstatic and spoke of "miracles" and "gifts from God." He pulled Leanna out of school but he treated her like a little country princess. And, somehow, he convinced us all it was for real. Convinced us that his sudden rages and violent fits were history and he was gentle again. Even Leanna seemed to believe he'd changed. He turned the sewing room into a nursery, all painted in pinks and blues and teddy bears.

He and my mother delivered the baby themselves, and despite Leanna never seeing a doctor once in the entire pregnancy, my little sister was born pink and healthy. I knew she was the fruit of a horrible sin against Leanna, but I fell in love with the baby right away. She was a little blonde angel who looked up to me, *me* of all people, as someone important. I *mattered*, finally. I had never been so happy as when I got to feed her and hold her.

Father let Leanna go back to school, riding the bus with me into town. She was relieved to be out in the world again. I couldn't wait to get back home to play with the baby.

Yet one day, we got home and ... the nursery wasn't there. The crib and toys were gone, replaced once again with my mother's sewing machine and cabinets of cloth and thread. In the space between morning and evening, pink and blue walls had become a flat, mute green. To this day, the smell of fresh paint makes me nauseated.

I ran to my mother with Leanna close behind and said, "Where's the baby?"

And, God save her soul, our mother wiped the dishwater off her hands, looked me dead in my eyes and said with a gasping little laugh, "Don't be silly, dear. There's no baby here."

Our mother stepped closer, lowering her voice to the faintest whisper. "There was *never* any baby here, understand? That's how this has to be."

Leanna wilted. In her dry eyes I could see her soul collapsing, and she simply went to her room and shut the door like a good girl.

My brain completely short-circuited. I lost all sense of self-preservation. I ran into my father's art room where he was sketching yet another Aryan Jesus and I screamed, "What did you do to my baby sister?"

He got up from his chair and with a priestlike calm punched me right in the face. I went down like a sack of wet sand, my lip and nose bleeding, teeth feeling loose in my aching jaw.

He stared down at me like I was something his coon hound vomited on the carpet. "Don't you ever raise your voice to me again, girl. Get to your room and don't come out 'til you're called out."

I went to my room and wept for hours. When crying wasn't enough to release the horrible black ocean in my soul, I started tearing the room apart, screaming and breaking anything that would smash. My father came in and told me that if I wanted something to cry about, he would give it to me. He twisted my arm right out of my shoulder socket, and that evening he taught me that it was possible to endure incredible pain in perfect silence.

And so I was perfectly silent as I stared down at the old doorknob, the hooked memories climbing the walls of my skull. If I opened the door, what would I find beyond? But just as my fingers closed around the tarnished brass, I heard my father speak my name, summoning me like a sorcerer calling up an obedient demon.

"You gonna come say hello to me, Maybelle?"

"Yes, Dad, I'll be there in a moment." My voice sounded like my mother's inside my own head.

I turned away from the door and went into the living room like any good daughter. My father was there in his favorite chair, his hair and beard looking a little greyer perhaps but really he was just about the same as when I'd last set eyes on him.

"How are things out your way?" he asked. His hands were folded in his lap and his soft flannel shirt made him look huggable. Kindly and gentle. He did not look like a rapist. He did not look like the man who had dislocated my arm and threatened to kill me. He did not look like a man who would erase the existence of his own child.

"It's very pretty this time of year," I replied. "Lots of wildflowers."

"That's good," he said. "A girl like you deserves to live in a place of God's beauty."

"How long has Leanna been sick?" I asked.

"I reckon she lived with it a long while now. It's a terrible thing," he said. "We're all terrible broke up about it."

There was a faint, strange odor in the room that I couldn't quite place. It mostly smelled like rust and rotten wood, but it also contained a sharp chemical note like burnt plastic. What could it be? Old mold and fungicide? Glue? I looked around at the ivy-colored carpet and the wisteria-patterned wallpaper for signs of water damage or a recent remodeling, but everything seemed just the same as when I called this place home.

A feline head butted against my calf. I glanced down, and saw a white and gray kitty who looked a whole lot like my old cat Mouser. He rubbed against me, purring, and I picked him up and set him on my lap.

My head spun as I stared into the cat's face and realized that he didn't just look a whole lot like Mouser ... he *was* Mouser. His mismatched green and blue eyes, the deep scar on his left ear from a fight with a raccoon ... he was the same as he'd been at his prime. But he'd gotten sick with feline leukemia when I was nine, and I'd buried him myself.

This cat had been dead for a quarter of a century, and yet there he was, purring and kneading on my lap. He was soft, very soft, just the way I remembered. I looked around the room. All of it was exactly the way I remembered.

A clammy dread filled me. I stared at my father, who was smiling at me benevolently.

"Where am I? Where am I, *really*?"

"Why, you're home, Maybelle. You're home where you belong."

I gently set Mouser down on the carpet and stood up.

"Where are you going?" my father asked. "Sit down, relax. Your mother will bring us some tea."

"I have to check on something." I turned away from him and headed down the hall to Leanna's old bedroom.

My father hurried after me. "Now, don't go in there, she's resting."

"I won't wake her." Keeping my mind as neutral as possible, I opened the door.

Leanna's room was just the way I remembered it. She lay in bed, fast asleep, looking just the way she had when she was recovering from a bad case of the flu.

And here, in this careful recreation of my home, she was still a teenager, not a woman pushing forty.

I turned, dodged past the thing pretending to be my father, and ran to the sewing room.

49

As my fingers closed around the brass knob, the father-thing shouted, "No, don't go in there, it's a horrible mess in there!"

I pushed open the door, not knowing whether I'd see my mother's workshop or the pink-and-blue nursery –

– but instead I found myself standing in my own bedroom, staring at my own twelve-year-old self. My young face was bruised, streaked with tears. A rage that was far too big for my small body to hold contorted my features. Twelve-me had smashed apart all the furniture, and gripped a broken chair leg like a club.

"I HATE YOU!" She swung the chair leg at my head with both hands.

The wood connected solidly with my temple. My vision exploded in white, and my legs collapsed under me. I'd barely gotten my sight back before Twelve-me started beating the shit out of me with the improvised club.

"You're worthless!" she shouted down at me. "You could have done something, but you didn't do anything! You just covered your ears and pretended it was all fine!"

She screamed all the terrible things I'd secretly believed about myself on my worst nights. Hearing them out loud was like hearing holy judgment on my soul. I balled up on the floor, covering my head with my arms. Twelve-me continued to pound away, striking a numbing, agonizing blow on the nerve bundle behind my elbow. The next blow sent sparks of pain across my whole body.

She would kill me if I didn't defend myself. I grabbed the club on the next downswing and tried to wrestle it away from her. But the chair leg sprouted tiny itchy vines like kudzu. They sprawled over my hands and arms, snaring me.

I bucked and fought to get myself free while Twelve-me hit me with her narrow fists. Then father-thing stepped into the room. Twelve-me ceased her attack and stood up, waiting.

Father-thing stared down at me with a look of profound disappointment and contempt. "You should have done as you were told, girl."

Mother-thing came in behind him, wiping her hands on her apron, blankly gazing off into space. "'Obey your parents in all things, for this is well pleasing unto the Lord'."

Their expressions didn't change as their bodies spasmed, dark green tendrils bursting through their pale skins. They collapsed, their flesh disintegrating and reweaving into writhing kudzu, vines joining vines that slithered over my limbs and held me down on the floor.

Twelve-me fell on top of me, suddenly serene as a graveyard angel. Her face and arms had grown impossibly long. Black kudzu leaves slit through her skin like necrotic tongues.

"Stop struggling and we can go eat mother's supper. Stop struggling and it'll all be just like it should have been." Her voice was the hiss of rain on pine needles and dry bones, gentle and mesmerizing. "You'll stay here where you belong. It'll all be fine; be a good girl and do what you're told ...."

The room went dark. It would have been so easy to give in. It would have been so easy to agree to the death the creature offered me: peace, at last, and forgiveness for my sin of surviving.

But instead I screamed and fought. The floor beneath me had disappeared into rough dirt and the viny monster was trying to drag me under. I struggled as hard as I could and got my good arm free, reaching for something, *anything,* that I could grab to get myself out of there.

A flashlight beam cut the gloom.

"Maybelle!" Alonzo shouted.

"Here!" I waved my free hand frantically.

"I can't get to you!" he hollered back.

I pushed up with all my strength and reached out to him. Vines popped loose from the dirt. He grabbed my hand in his strong wiry grip and pulled. The vines held fast to my trapped limbs. I thought they would pull my shoulder right out of its socket again. But green wood gave before my flesh did, and I lurched to my feet in a cloud of dust and ash.

Alonzo and I ran like hell for his taxi. The black kudzu seemed to be exploding out of the ground all around us, vines writhing and flailing, hissing through the pine needles and leaves as they tried to snare our legs.

We made it back to the rusty gate, threw ourselves over the bars, and scrambled into his cab, me in the passenger seat, both of us gasping for breath. He tore out of there and neither of us said anything at all until we were miles down the highway.

A rest stop appeared around the next bend, friendly and bright. He pulled into the parking lot beneath one of the lights. The blue glow felt like safety.

"That thing wanted you bad." Alonzo's voice shook like my body. "I saw ... I saw you in the house, but I could see through it, and those vines ..."

He shuddered. "I saw those people ... what were they, ghosts?"

I shook my head numbly. "Bait. Just bait."

Then I took a harder look at him. "How did you know to come back? I didn't call you. I *couldn't* call you."

"When I dropped you off, that place just gave me the creeps, you know? So I did a web search on the address. And there was ... there was a fire five years ago. The house ... it burned down with everyone inside."

"What? Let me see."

Alonzo pulled the news story up on his cell phone. "There's all kind of jagged metal and holes and stuff in a place like that, and I thought I should check on you. My aunt would never let me hear the end of it if I left a customer someplace I knew was dangerous and they got hurt."

I took the phone from him. It displayed a photo of the charred ruin of my father's house. The article beneath said someone had doused the place in kerosene and lit it with a cigarette. Firefighters found three adult bodies in the wreckage, all burned down to bones and teeth. Arson investigators discovered the skeleton of an infant in the dirt beneath the porch. She had died of a skull fracture; either someone dropped her or someone strong had hit her just once.

"Oh, baby," I whispered. Part of me had held onto some slight hope that my parents gave her up for adoption. Tears streamed down my face. "Oh, Leanna."

My big sister had gone home to get her own closure, but something terrible and hungry had been born in the blood and ashes and lingering nightmares.

"I'm so sorry," Alonzo said. "I ... I can't believe nobody called to tell you what happened."

I shrugged miserably. "How could they? Almost nobody knew me when I did live here, and that was long ago."

I wiped my eyes, turned and fixed Alonzo in a hard gaze. "Were you serious when you said you wanted to make the world a better place for everyone?"

He swallowed nervously. "Yes, ma'am. I am dead serious about that."

"That thing you saw? It's still alive up there. If it can't have me, I bet it'll settle for somebody else. You think any of the folks in your aunt's church would be willing to grab some machetes and blow torches and do a little weed control come sunup?"

He nodded. "Yes, ma'am, I believe they would."

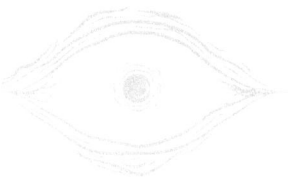

The Cold Gallery

Emma and her mother joined the line of kids and parents in Riggleman Hall's foyer. They'd be waiting a while. The Freshman Orientation coordinators had scheduled far too few advisors for far too many students.

Suddenly, a chill crept across Emma's back, and she felt a pair of icy hands close around her neck.

"Hey!" She whirled around.

"What's the matter?" Her mom looked puzzled.

"Someone..." Emma trailed off. Not only was nobody standing behind her, nobody was within twenty feet of her. "Nothing. Just my nerves, I guess."

"Well, this is nice." Emma's mother led the way into the dorm room and plunked down the duffel bag. "*Very* nice, don't you think?"

"Um." Emma set down her suitcases. The relentlessly beige room was smaller than it had looked on the university website. At least she had the place to herself. "Yeah, it seems nice, Mom."

"The dorms we had weren't nearly this spacious."

Looking wistful, her mom opened her purse and pulled out the letter from her father, Professor Burke.

Her father. It felt weird to even think the words. It was easier to think of him as the Professor. Growing up, the other kids at her school had fathers or stepfathers or erstwhile "uncles", but never Emma. She couldn't even remember her mom ever going on a date. Of course, with her grindingly long shifts at the hospital, it was hard for her to have much of a social life.

And that, at least according to her Aunt Mary, was entirely her father's fault.

Emma's mom rarely spoke of him, but her aunt wasn't one to mince words or keep silent. According to Mary, her father was Edgar Burke, a chemistry instructor who dumped her mother when she got pregnant. Emma's mom had to drop out of college and go to work as a nurses' aide while he went on to become a full professor with a fat salary. Mary wanted her sister to sue for child support, but Emma's mother never followed up with the lawyers Mary contacted on her behalf.

It seemed the good Professor was determined to have nothing to do with his daughter. But on her 16th birthday, a FedEx guy delivered a fancy basket of Godiva chocolates to their little clapboard rental in Huntington. That night, Burke telephoned the house, and Emma had her first, awkward conversation with the man who until that day had only given her half her genes.

The support checks came Johnny-on-the-spot after that. And on her next birthday, right when Emma and her mother were starting to fret over college costs, he offered to pay for Emma to attend UC.

"Your father wants to meet with you in his office at noon tomorrow," her mom said, reading over the letter. "He's in Clay Tower."

Emma suddenly felt nervous. She'd talked to the Professor at most six times on the phone, and he'd been away at a conference when she and her mom visited the campus before. "Are ... are you going to come with me?"

Her mother's smile faded for the briefest second. "No, honey, I ... I have to be back at the hospital tomorrow. Look, it'll be fine! Just be your regular sweet self. We can thank the Lord that he's changed his ways and found the love of Jesus in his heart to finally do right by you."

There were no crosses in Professor Burke's office. Nor were there any Christian books that Emma could see in the floor-to-ceiling oak shelves that lined every inch of wall space beyond the doorway and wide window. The *Encyclopedia Paranormal* volumes and books on Voudun and Medieval witchcraft scattered amongst the organic chemistry and mathematics texts counted as a sort of religious reading, Emma supposed, but surely not the kind that involved Jesus or love.

The professor himself was sitting behind a wide desk, engrossed in a science journal. He was a lean, well-kept man in his late 40s or early 50s, and he was dressed much more stylishly than she'd expected. His handsome face was an odd mix of the strange and familiar: his nose and full lips were masculine versions of hers, and she'd seen his gray eyes in every mirror.

Emma wiped her sweaty palms on her khaki skirt and cleared her throat. Burke finally looked up and noticed her standing in the doorway. His face broke into a smile as broad and bright as the noon sun over Antarctica.

"You must be Emma," he said, standing and gesturing toward one of the high-backed chairs in front of his desk. "Please, come in and have a seat. So, you're settled in the dormitory okay? Got all the classes you wanted to take?"

"Yes sir," she said as she sat down.

"Good, good." He opened one of his desk drawers and pulled out a sheet of paper. "I took the liberty of getting you a job here on campus at the Erma Byrd Art Gallery. It's just ten hours a week, and they'll work around your schedule. I'm sure you could use a bit of pocket money, and it will look good on your resume."

He passed the paper to her. It was a job acceptance letter signed by the museum curator. All official and addressed to her, just as if she'd applied on her own. She was going to be an evening attendant, whatever that meant.

The art gallery was in Riggleman Hall; the tall, dark windows striping the building seemed much more ominous than they had the day before. Inside, it felt like the building's AC was cranked up too high, although students jostling past her on the first floor were complaining about the heat. Emma took the stairs to try to warm up, but she felt even colder by the time she got to the gallery.

The curator, Mrs. Plymale, was a bright, cheery woman in her mid-30s.

"What you'll mostly be doing is keeping an eye on things and answering questions," she told Emma. "I'll give you a packet of information about all our artists and the paintings on display. It's usually pretty quiet here, but we'll give you a walkie-talkie in case you need to call maintenance or security. Also, we have special events like weddings on some weekends, and we'll need help setting up and tearing down. Nothing very hard or intense."

Emma had been rubbing her arms to try to warm them a little. Mrs. Plymale seemed to notice her goosebumps.

"Is it cold to you in here?" the curator asked. She was wearing a light, sleeveless dress. There was a faint sheen of perspiration at the base of her neck.

Emma nodded. "A little."

Mrs. Plymale smiled sympathetically. "It's like that for some people who are ... *sensitive*, I guess is the best word. My advice is, don't stay too long after your shift is over. It might be worse after dark."

"Worse? How?"

Mrs. Plymale held up both hands. "Mind you, I haven't felt anything weird myself, so I don't put *that* much stock in stories of this place being haunted. But people have sworn they've heard voices, felt strange touches and cold spots. Things like that. Mostly after sunset."

"The building is haunted? By *what*?"

The curator laughed uncomfortably. "There's a story that a girl died. Killed herself when she found out she was pregnant. Some people say she jumped off the roof, others say she poisoned herself. Lots of rumors, not much evidence. They wouldn't be able to keep a student's death out of the papers nowadays, but decades ago … well, who knows what might have happened here?"

Emma's first shift in the gallery was deadly slow. Two visitors came her first hour, and nobody after that. She'd brought a cotton jacket with her, but even so the chill got to her after a while and so she spent the last hour pacing up and down the glossy checkerboard floor, reading Mrs. Plymale's handout on West Virginia Women Artists.

Afterward, she decided to take the stairs back to the ground floor. The hallway door had just shut behind her on the landing when she thought she heard a whisper.

Blood for blood.

A wave of cold vertigo hit her, and suddenly she pitched forward, arms windmilling, barely able to catch herself on the safety rail. Trembling, she got to her feet, her wrenched shoulder aching sharply. She was alone; surely the disembodied voice had just been her imagination.

But her fall had been far from imaginary. If she'd missed that railing, she'd have gone headfirst down the stairs, probably breaking her neck in the process.

No more stairs for her, not if she could help it.

Her next shift involved a few more visitors, but the last hour was just as quiet as before. She began to circle the gallery, looking at the paintings.

On her third circuit, she saw something on the wall she was sure hadn't been there before. It was a charcoal drawing in a battered round frame. It depicted a man and a woman watching a sunset from atop a square building with long, dark windows. Riggleman Hall, Emma realized. The drawing was amateur compared to the rest of the works in the gallery, but something about it kept her riveted.

The shivery vertigo took her again, and suddenly she was standing on the roof, gazing into the grey eyes of a handsome, wispy-bearded, shaggy-haired boy of 18 or 19. He wore a butterfly-collared green shirt and bell-bottoms.

He was shaking his head at her. "We can't have a kid, Linda. I'm not even close to being done with school; I can't be tied down right now. I'll drive you to Columbus; we can get it taken care of up there and your folks will never—"

"No," she heard herself say. "I'm havin' our baby, and you're gonna be a man for a change and do the right thing."

A cold, hard anger gleamed in his eyes. No love there. "You don't get to push me around, girl."

"Fine." She turned and began to walk away across the gravel rooftop. "We'll see what your Pa has to say."

Suddenly he grabbed her arm and jerked her sideways, nearly off her feet. Eddie was stronger than she'd expected, too strong to resist. In a heartbeat he'd thrown her off the building and she was tumbling through the air, the merciless concrete steps rising to meet her—

Emma was back in her own body, crumpled on the floor beneath the enchanted painting.

Blood for blood, the murdered girl's voice whispered inside her head. *If I can't have him, I'll take you.*

Emma felt the ghost's tormented emotions burning like rattlesnake venom in her veins. The pain of betrayal. Rage over her destroyed future, lost motherhood, forgotten name. And blind hatred for Emma, her murdering lover's child, the adored daughter of the relationship that should have been hers—

"No," Emma gasped, her heart twitching jaggedly in her chest. "That's not how it's been. Please, listen."

She opened her memories to the ghost, praying Linda wasn't so bent on vengeance she wouldn't care about the truth....

"Come in; it's not locked."

Professor Burke looked supremely surprised to see his daughter push open his office door.

"Emma? I didn't expect—"

"—that I'd still be alive? Us girls, we're full of surprises, huh? Can't count on us to save you from thirty-year-old blood curses or *anything*."

"What?"

"I really appreciate being used as ghost bait, *Dad*. And Linda, she sure appreciates being murdered."

The color had drained from his face. "I'm sure I don't know what you're talking about."

"Really? Maybe this will jog your memory."

She pulled Linda's drawing from its hiding place under her jacket and turned the image toward her father.

At least fifty people crowded outside the police tape surrounding Professor Burke's broken body at the base of Clay Tower: tired-looking EMTs, grim-faced cops, whispering faculty, and students surreptitiously filming the carnage with their cell phones.

"... so you're saying he threw the chair through his window, and jumped out after it?" the police detective asked Emma.

"Yes sir."

"And he didn't say why?"

"I ... didn't know my father very well," she replied. "Maybe something was bothering him that he never talked about."

"Maybe." The detective flipped his notebook closed. "In any case, I'm sorry for your loss, Miss."

In a strange way, Emma realized, so was she.

Abandonment Option

Martin Bennington graduated at the top of his Harvard MBA class, sat on the boards of the noblest charities, dined at the most lavish restaurants, bedded the most beautiful models, and ran the best-respected investment firm on Wall Street.

Now, he was standing naked before a bored Bureau of Prisons officer at the Lynchwood Federal Correctional Institution. The gray, vinyl-tiled floor was simultaneously gritty and sticky underneath his bare feet.

"Lift up your scrotum," ordered the officer.

Martin did as he was told, chagrined to see how far his penis had retreated from the chilly room. He also wondered what any man could possibly hide behind his testicles. A file? A knife? Plastic explosives? That would take quite a pair.

"Turn around, bend over, and spread your cheeks."

His lawyer had advised him to go to his "happy place" once those words were uttered. Martin was a man who usually liked to live in the moment. And so, as unfriendly gloved fingers probed his most tender places, it was difficult to imagine he'd ever spent pleasant days entertaining starlets at the Isle of Capri and Bora Bora, but he closed his eyes and did his best.

Finally, the strip-search was over, and the officer told him to gather up his clothes. He led Martin into another room where he received a pair of tan polyester prison pants and matching shirt along with scratchy white underwear, undershirt and socks. Tacky slip-on sneakers completed the ensemble. Martin gave his street clothes to the receiving clerk, who dropped them into a cardboard box that would be shipped back to Martin's wife. She probably wouldn't even notice the delivery; she was too busy fending off the Feds in an effort to keep the Florida mansion he'd put in her name. The media probably weren't helping, either.

After getting dressed and signing off on the inventory form, the guards took Martin to yet another room where he was photographed for his prison ID card and then fingerprinted. A male nurse came in with more paperwork but no blood pressure cuff or stethoscope.

"How's your health?" asked the nurse, not looking up from the clipboard.

"Fit as a fiddle," Martin lied.

Not quite twelve months before, Martin was sitting in his doctor's office.

"You know the fatigue you've been feeling, and the shortness of breath you've been experiencing at the gym?"

Martin nodded, already suspecting and fearing the answer.

"The tests confirmed it's congestive heart failure: your heart muscle has gotten stiff and so the chambers aren't filling like they should. It's causing fluid to back up in your lungs. But I don't want you to panic … this is treatable. We're going to keep you on the Lotensin but also put you on Lasix, which is a diuretic that should help reduce a lot of your symptoms.

"Your diet's really important here," his doctor continued. "Stick to chicken and fish and eat lots of veggies. And I really want you to watch your salt intake. If I see you eating any more caviar canapés down at the country club, I'm going to kick your well-insured ass from here to Honolulu. If your ticker gets worse, we'll have to find you a replacement—and even with *your* resources, that won't be easy."

"I'll watch my diet," Martin said, lifting his hand with three fingers raised. "Scout's honor."

Before reporting for his 10-year prison sentence, Martin had his driver take him to a nearby steakhouse, where he dropped what was left of his pocket money on a lunch of fried shrimp and a thick New York strip. He limited himself to a single glass of mediocre Bordeaux; his lawyer had warned of dire consequences if he showed up at the FCI even slightly inebriated.

The briny red meat had worked its way into his blood, and his vision twitched with every beat of his straining heart.

"For some reason, we haven't received your PSI paperwork yet." The unit manager handed Martin a package of flimsy white towels and sheets topped with a package of basic toiletries. The manager's hands shook ever so slightly, and Martin saw a few drops of sweat on the man's tanned brow. "So you'll have to go to the

Secure Housing Unit until we get those documents and can finish processing you. Then you'll be transferred to the Camp dorm."

Martin slipped his fingers inside the towel stack to ensure that the object he'd requested was there, then indulged in a grim smile. If his lawyers had done their jobs, he'd never have to see the inside of the inmate dormitory, and he'd have to endure the cell for a few hours at the most. He took a deep breath, trying to steady himself for what was going to happen next ....

"Money isn't everything," his father had told him once they were ensconced in the back of the limo after Martin's MBA graduation ceremony. "Luck matters a whole lot more in this world. If you have enough luck, the money comes practically on its own. The thing that they probably didn't tell you in those fancy economics classes of yours is that the phenomenon we call luck is actually a commodity just like everything else. It can be bought and sold, although only a fool sells off his own luck."

The elder Bennington drained his martini glass down to the olive; Martin was quick to pour the old man another from the limousine's wet bar. The old man grinned. "Do you think you're ready to find out why our family has been so damn lucky?"

Something in his father's tone sent a chill up young Martin's spine. "Of course I am, Dad."

His father laughed and steadied his drink with a practiced hand as the driver slammed the accelerator and the limo lurched up the I-84 onramp. "Of course you think you're ready. When I was your age, I was ready to drink the whisky barrels dry, ready to fuck a thousand girls, ready to take Wall Street by the balls and make 'em all beg for mercy. But I was most definitely not ready to see what my father showed me. What I'm going to show you tonight. We'll see what you're made of after that."

Once they were back at the family mansion in Westport, Martin's father took him into his study.

"Someone once said that sufficiently advanced technology is indistinguishable from magic," his father said as he pulled some old leather-bound law texts off one of his polished bookshelves to reveal a keypad behind them. "I would disagree with that; once you've seen magic—the real kind, not that David Copperfield bullshit—you're not going to confuse it with a Cray or a jumbo jet."

The old man finished punching in a long string of numbers, and one of the bookshelves at the back of the room emitted a click and swung a few inches away from the wall.

"But I will make a truer version of that statement: possessing sufficient amounts of accurate information becomes indistinguishable from possessing an unusual amount of luck." Martin's father crossed the room to the bookshelf door and swung it wide, revealing an old iron door that looked like it might go down to a cellar. "Go to Atlantic City and sit down at the poker tables—if you know exactly how the cards will fall, you'll break every bastard in the room. Go to Wall Street—if you know how the markets will swing five months, ten months, ten years down the road—well. You'll do pretty well for yourself, won't you?"

"But that's ... not possible, is it?" Martin said.

His father laughed and dug in the inside breast pocket of his tuxedo, producing a wrought-iron key. "It is very much possible, son. But I'm not talking about the kind of information that ordinary people—even your fancy Harvard mathematics whiz kids—could ever get their hands on."

He put the key in the heavy lock and opened the forbidding door with some effort. "I know of exactly one source in the whole world for that kind of information, and you're about to meet him."

Martin followed his father down marble steps into a subterranean room lit with old-fashioned gaslight sconces. Near the door, there was an old oak table littered with various arcane-looking implements, but the room was completely dominated by what sat at the far end: a golden skeleton on some kind of throne. Even though the metal bones glittered, they also seemed to draw the light from the room.

"Meet the man John D. Rockefeller once said was the most skilled businessman he'd ever known," Martin's father said. "Or what his dusty corpse became, anyhow."

"That's Gould?" Martin asked, incredulous. "Jay Gould, the robber baron?"

Martin stepped closer to the precious revenant. Its skull had polished rubies in the eye sockets. The top of the cranium bore a threaded screw hole. There was a buildup of some kind of dried, tarry substance that, when liquid, had apparently spilled down from the foramen magnum over the spinal column and the ribs, staining a dark pool on the red velvet seat of the throne.

"Now, don't call the old boy names," his father said, a perverse smile playing on his face. "He still has feelings, you know. *Pride*, anyhow. Best to stay on his good side if you want his help. And believe me, son, you *do* want his help."

"But ... how ...." A million questions were jostling in Martin's head, and he found himself unable to articulate a single one of them.

"How, indeed," his father said, looking tremendously amused at Martin's confusion. "About fifteen years after Jay Gould died, your grandfather met a prospective business partner, a nephew of King Carol of Romania, who claimed to have a plan for generating great riches for them both. The pair of them broke into Gould's mausoleum, replaced his remains with the corpse of a peasant, and smuggled Jay's body out to a monastery in the Carpathians where the monks were known to be skilled in, well, *certain mysteries*. Once your grandfather acquired all the gold and jewels necessary for the ritual, the monks gilded and enchanted the skeleton as if it were a holy relic, summoning and binding Jay's soul to the bones and giving it clairvoyance into all possible futures.

"When Jay's skeleton was completed, the king's nephew of course tried to double-cross your grandfather and have him murdered, but he was too tough and far too sly to fall for that kind of a trick. Your grandfather took the skeleton for himself, and hightailed back to the States. Old Jay's been down here ever since.

"The throne was my idea," his father continued. "Jay wasn't too happy with your grandfather after a while, and so I got him the chair as sort of a peace offering when I took over. It belonged to King Louis XIV of France ... it's not magic, but it is a very fine place to sit."

"What's that black stuff on the bones and seat?" Martin asked.

"Blood," his father replied. "Even spirits need to eat. I can get an answer with, say, fresh chicken blood, but old Jay always did have a taste for human juice."

Martin's father leaned over the cluttered table and picked up a bronze funnel with a threaded tip, a bronze dish, and a very sharp-looking silver dagger. "I haven't fed him in a while, so he's sleeping now, but I might as well get you two introduced. Give me your hand, son ...."

Two guards flanked Martin as he carried his pack of linens and towels down the gray hall to the Secure Housing Unit. Most of the men crammed by twos and threes in the 8'x10' cells were dressed in bright orange jumpsuits. At the far end was a cell occupied by one young, worried-looking man in the same tan clothing Martin had been issued. The young fellow's skin was fair, but his broad nose and close-cropped curly hair spoke of a mixed ethnic ancestry. His solemn green eyes blinked behind thick glasses.

"Hey, any word on my paperwork?" the young man called out to the guards.

"No paperwork, but we brought you a new bunky," one of the guards replied. They marched Martin up to the cell, unlocked it, and put him inside. "You boys play nice, y'hear?"

"Whoa." The gangly young man's eyes widened. "Are you Bennington?"

Martin set his stack of towels and linens on the small desk. "That I am."

"Oh, wow, it's an honor, sir ... I mean, the circumstances aren't—look, you can take the bottom bunk, a man like you shouldn't have to climb up on this rickety thing."

"Thank you," Martin said, unfolding one of the steel chairs and taking a seat. "But don't worry about all that now. Tell me about yourself."

"Uh, my name's Raymond Greene, and I used to work for Groshawk Investments. I was only there eleven months. I got a job there right out of college. I thought I had it made, but...." His voice faltered.

"Did you get caught in the embezzlement scam Hobson was running?" Martin asked gently.

"Yes," Raymond replied, looking profoundly depressed. His glasses were slipping down his nose, and he pushed them up with a long forefinger. "And I know this makes me sound like a liar or an idiot, but I had *no* idea what was going on. Those papers they found ... they had my signature on them, but I know I never saw those docs before the trial. And that money that showed up in my bank account ... I had no idea. It's like I got set up, but there's no reason to set up a guy like me, so my own lawyer didn't even believe me."

"Well, my lawyer's pretty good, not to mention open-minded; maybe I can get him to look at your case," Martin said.

"You'd do that? Wow, thanks, bro. Sir, I mean."

Martin smiled. "Always glad to help out a fellow in need."

"What, um ... what about you, sir? I mean, I know they convicted you and all, but was the prosecution telling the truth?"

"Parts of it," Martin replied.

"What about the hedge fund? Was it *ever* legit, or was it a Ponzi from the start like they said?"

"It started as a legitimate thing," Martin lied. "Things just ... got out of hand. It's hard to give up on that kind of money; you just keep hoping the tide will turn before it's too late."

Martin hadn't needed anything as flimsy as hope. He knew going in exactly what would happen; he'd started the scam to feather his nest against the impending economic collapse Jay Gould's ghost had foreseen. His reputation had been ruined and he'd been sent to prison, but he'd achieved his ultimate goal. For every dollar the feds had confiscated, there was another ten hidden as well-protected caches of precious metals and weapons around the country.

"Sixty billion is a lot to walk away from," Raymond agreed. "And you had, what, four hundred million in liquid assets?"

"About that, yes."

"So why didn't you ... you know, disappear?"

The young man's shyness finally seemed to be falling away. It was about damn time, Martin figured. The timid didn't belong on Wall Street, and Martin hated to think the kid had taken a good job away from someone more competent, even if the ship *was* going down.

"I mean, people have killed themselves over the money they lost. There are angry mothers and fathers and husbands and wives out there. Angry mobsters, too, I heard." Raymond leaned in close, lowering his voice to a whisper. "When I was on the prison bus, I heard some talk about how there's a hit out on you. And you have to have heard that, too. So why didn't you run?"

"That's a little complicated," Martin said.

A few hours after Martin got his congestive heart failure diagnosis, he went down into the secret cellar to talk to Jay. It had been a while since he'd consulted his silent partner. Once he'd poured a half-pint of fresh blood (courtesy of a local med tech on his payroll) into the golden skull, the skeleton's ruby eyes lit up with the faint smoky fire that let him know Mr. Gould was awake and ready to talk.

"You told me that there was only a 10% chance my heart would start to fail," Martin said, his arms crossed.

"I'm sorry that mortality is touching you so soon, but a 10% chance is not the same as a zero chance," the skeleton replied. Its thin voice seemed to be nowhere and everywhere.

"What am I supposed to do now?"

"Stick with the plan you've set in motion. Only now, your goal will be securing your daughters' futures. You'll need to step aside as your father did and pick one of them to introduce to me."

Martin shook his head. "I'm not ready. I don't want to step aside, I don't want to go to prison, not even for a day. Surely—surely Japan or Switzerland have better treatments, better access to fresh hearts."

"You'll be apprehended in any country with a decent medical system. And you'll die in any that don't. Medicine will have a cure for what ails you, but not for another ten years. And there's a 40% chance they'll *never* have a cure if the collapse comes. I feel your pain, Martin, really I do ... a shot of cheese mold extract would have kept me from dying of consumption, but the doctors in my day couldn't figure out something as simple as that."

"What can I do, sir? Is there *anything* I can do?"

"You can reverse course and come clean to the authorities, if you want. It'll cost your family their fortune, but the fraud we've engineered has added 15% to the probability that the nation will collapse. If you reverse the economic damage, things may stabilize. And then, you have a 60% chance of pleading down to probation if you pay back all the money, and if that happens you'll be very likely to die in your eighties, as your father did. Comfortable, once again a respected pillar of the community, forgiven of your sins in society's eyes, provided you can resist the temptation to sell me off."

Martin almost said "I wouldn't sell you," but clearly Jay knew what lay in the basement of his heart. It did no good to lie to his deathly confidante.

"So I come clean and maybe get thirty more years of living," Martin mused. "What's thirty years?"

"To many, it is a lifetime," the skeleton observed.

"But in the grand scheme, it's nothing," Martin replied, pacing. "All my money, all my power, gone, like *that*. And then what? To be mostly forgotten in fifty years, entirely forgotten in two hundred?"

"I don't know what lies beyond," Jay replied. "I surely tasted it before I was bound to these bones, but I cannot remember whether I took my leisure in Heaven, suffered in Hell, or simply waited in darkness."

"I can't count on a happy afterlife, not after everything I've done. Is there any other option for me here? Is there a way ... to continue?"

The skeleton was silent for a moment. "I do know of a way you could become immortal, but be warned that it involves great sacrifice and the blackest of magic. Among other debasements, you will have to spill the heart's blood of your close kin, and then do worse. One of your daughters would do."

Martin flinched. "I couldn't murder one of my babies. They're spoiled little brats like their mother most of the time and I'll be damned if I want to hand my companies over to them ... but I could never hurt either one of them." He took a deep breath. "Would anyone else fit the bill?"

"As a matter of fact, yes; there are others, and one in particular who can best be put to use...."

"On second thought, maybe the question of why I didn't run away isn't so complicated after all," Martin said to Raymond. "Ultimately, I knew that trying to escape to another country wouldn't work out so well for me, whether there's a bounty on my life or not."

"What are you going to do to protect yourself?" Raymond asked.

"Nothing," Martin replied.

In response to Raymond's shocked expression, he replied: "Now, don't get me wrong, I'm not suicidal—I love life and being alive. *Love* it. Maybe I'm not quite as indulgent as my father. He loved his drink, and he loved his women, right to the end. He was still tomcatting around in his seventies, and he even fathered a son the rest of us never knew about. You, in fact."

It took a moment for Martin's words to sink in. "W-what? You mean I'm—"

"My half-brother. Exactly! Nice to finally meet you, half-brother!" Martin clapped him on the arm.

Raymond seemed dumbfounded, so Martin continued, speaking fast as a salesman. "It might seem like an amazing coincidence we'd encounter each other in prison, but let me tell you, I took great pains to make sure we'd meet right in this very cell. All told, I must have paid out two million dollars in bribes to prison officials, FBI agents, forgers, and the recruiting director and your bosses at Groshawk, all so we'd be able to spend a little quality time together."

Raymond's mouth hung open, and for the first time, Martin saw a definite family resemblance: two of his lower front teeth overlapped crookedly, just as his father's had.

Martin reached into his towel stack and quickly pulled out the silver dagger planted by the bribed unit manager and—in a motion he'd practiced a thousand times over the past year—he slashed the scalpel-sharp blade across his brother's throat. Raymond's hands went to his neck as his carotid artery began to jet out, but Martin didn't flinch, didn't pause, simply shoved the kid down onto the concrete floor and quickly began smearing the magic symbols with bloodied fingers, chanting the words Jay had taught him, and when the symbols were complete and Raymond was twitching and gurgling horribly, there wasn't a moment to lose. Martin ripped open Raymond's scarlet-soaked shirt and carved into the taut flesh of the kid's upper abdomen to get at his heart from beneath. He grabbed the slippery pulsing muscle with his fingers, and his own heart was straining, aching sympathetically in his own chest when he finally managed to cut and tear the organ free. He shouted the last of the incantation, and took a bite of his half-brother's still-shuddering flesh and swallowed it like a chunk of unusually tough carpaccio.

The ritual was done, and the guard outside was shouting for help, fumbling with the keys, and when they finally got inside Martin screeched at them like a madman and flung himself at their knees. They hit him with their batons, and another primed his Taser and shot the electrified darts into Martin's back. The sudden current overwhelmed his weakened heart, and he felt himself sinking down, down into blackness.

When Martin came to, his bones hurt so much it seemed like they were on fire. He was able to hear before he was able to see, and when he tried to blink to clear his blurred vision, he discovered he couldn't move.

"Ask it a question," a young voice said.

"Shush! It needs tribute first," said another.

Something warm and delicious was pouring into him from the top of his head, and for a moment he could imagine it was a fine cocktail going down his throat, and not a cup of hot salty gore trickling through what was left of him, tarring the shining cage of bone that enclosed the dusty nothingness where his heart and guts used to live.

His ruby eyes focused, and he saw a muscular, battle-scarred young man standing before him in a motley of salvaged leathers and rough homespuns. A few other feral-looking youngsters lurked behind. Martin instantly knew everything about this hard youth: barely out of his teens, he'd already slaughtered a hundred men, but along with his sociopathic blood-lust he had a cunning intelligence. More important, his belly was fired with a thirst for power beyond the ruined section of Pittsburgh he'd staked out as his own kingdom. The boy knew he was still just a gangster, but his aspirations weren't yet sharpened to their deadliest points.

"Skeleton," the youth ordered. "Tell me about the future."

The doors of perception opened inside Martin's enslaved mind, and he saw the cities on fire and the streets running red with the blood of the boy's foes. The speck of humanity that remained inside Martin cursed Jay Gould and wept at these visions, but the rest of him, the part that had wanted more and more and more, was grimly pleased. He'd see the race through until the bitter end, even if he was just a consultant.

"As you wish, Lord John," Martin replied. "What part of the future unwritten did you want to see?"

"All, skeleton," the boy replied. "Give me everything."

The Cold Blackness Between

Mary Keller was exhausted but elated when Karl's eyes finally flickered open. He rose up a little on his one good elbow, the plastic sheet crinkling beneath him.

"Mary?" he rasped. "Where'm I? Throat … hurts. Feel like … crap."

She smiled. His voice was rough, but it worked. His head had been torn off when he lost control of his motorcycle and wrapped it around a tree up in the mountains. She'd not been sure she'd gotten his vocal cords reconstructed properly.

"Rest now. You don't need to worry about a thing. You just need to get your strength back."

She leaned down over the antique feather bed and kissed his still-cold forehead. At least the sleet that had slicked the roads that night had also meant he'd been wearing his helmet with the visor down. He hadn't gotten anything worse than a bloody nose when his head went skittering down into the rocky ravine.

Shattered bones, punctured lungs, crushed organs and severed spines she could handle; damaged brains were hard. It was like trying to put custard back together. If she'd had to bring him back from a crushed skull, chances were she'd end up with a zombie on her hands that was only the barest revenant of the man she loved.

"What happened?" he asked, his eyes already fluttering into the sleep of the living.

She kissed him again, then straightened up and re-checked the position of the I.V. needle in his arm. Her hands were trembling; it was definitely time for breakfast. The saline-and-glucose drip was still three-quarters full. She'd put two units of O-negative blood into him during the night. He needed far more than that, but even if she'd replaced all his blood, he'd still be more dead than alive. It would be several days before his system recovered from the shock. For now, it was most important that she not let him dry out while she slept.

That the transfusion needle was steel was unfortunate but unavoidable; she'd made sure to put it in his good arm, where the steel's interference with the life magic would cause the least damage to her work. Nothing else in the room contained inorganic iron; the I.V. stand was aluminum, the furniture put together with wooden pegs, the light fixtures bronze, the wiring copper. That floor of the mansion had its own breaker switch, and she'd turned its electricity off before she'd started work. Electricity had an unpredictable effect on resurrections.

She snuffed out the candles surrounding the bed and set her tray of bandages, sutures and ceramic surgical instruments up on the vanity. In the old days, she'd had to use instruments made from wood, ivory, and glass. Her mother had taught her how to chip scalpel blades from broken windowpanes, which Mary had always found a deeply tedious task. Modern ceramics were a wonderful invention.

Mary's skills as a witch kept her in high demand as a healer, but she'd never hoped to work on Karl. Soon after they started seeing each other, she cast a ward on him to keep him from harm. Dogs would not bite him, bees would not sting him, drunks would not pick a fight with him. But the spell couldn't protect him from the laws of physics, so she added a divination element to warn her when he was getting into danger.

She'd been downstairs reading a potboiler mystery when she had a vision of Karl sliding sideways on the icy highway. She sped out to Pineytop Road to try to intercept Karl before he crashed ... but she couldn't get there quite fast enough. At least she was able to get his body into her trunk before anyone else passed by and saw the wreck. The bike was a total loss, and far too heavy for her to lift; she rolled it down out of sight in the ravine.

Mary pulled the covers up to Karl's bandaged neck and stumbled to the bedroom door. She locked it behind her to keep her lover from prying eyes and started down the stairs.

Yolanda, their housekeeper, came through the back door just as Mary got down the stairs. The younger woman's eyes widened when she saw Mary.

"My God, are you okay?" Yolanda exclaimed.

Mary looked down at herself. Her sweatshirt and jeans were smeared with Karl's blood. She'd been so focused on saving Karl that she hadn't noticed.

"I'm fine," Mary replied. "Some friends from the gym took me out to Lake Zurich for a party last night. We hit a deer on the way back, and I helped Joe pull it off the grille and carry it off the road. The car was wrecked; I only got home a little while ago."

"Mr. Barrington doesn't like you going out partying." Yolanda's tone was matter-of-fact.

Mary shrugged. "He knew who I was when he married me. He knows I won't stay at home by myself. If he wants me here, he can stop going off on so many business trips."

She brushed at the crusty stains on her sweatshirt. "I need to put on something clean—I'll be back down in a minute."

Mary trudged up to her bedroom on the third floor to change. She wondered how she was ever going to break the news of her affair to William. He was still more her employer than her husband. She'd started as his personal nurse, but when sex became a part of their relationship, he decided they should be married. She was fond of him ... but he was not a passionate man and never had been. And he had grown increasingly cold over the past year; he hardly spent time with her anymore.

Karl was passionate, and sweet, and damn fine company. She first laid eyes on him at the gym; he was tall and lean and the smell of him made her blood sing. Karl had been reluctant to get involved with a married woman, but he was just as attracted to her as she to he.

At first she told herself it was just a casual fling, but the more time she spent with him, the more she knew in her heart that she couldn't bear to be without him. And she could tell how uncomfortable he was about having to sneak around.

Karl deserved better than to be her dirty little secret. And William deserved her honesty. She didn't know how she could do right by both men, so for now all she could worry about was keeping Karl alive.

"Is Mr. Barrington still coming back from Mexico City next Wednesday?" Yolanda asked when Mary returned.

"That's his plan, last I heard." Five days would suffice to get Karl strong enough to move to his apartment for the remainder of his recuperation. She shuffled into the kitchen and got a few slices of sourdough from the breadbox.

"I'm starving, and I'm exhausted." Mary said. "Would you mind fixing me some breakfast?"

"Not at all." Yolanda set a skillet on the stove to heat.

Mary got a butter knife from the draining rack, found her jar of herb paste in the refrigerator, and sat down at the blond oak breakfast table. Yolanda made a face as Mary spread the thick, green-black paste on the bread.

"I don't see how you can eat that stuff." Yolanda carried a bowl of oranges to the juicing machine. "It smells like shit."

"It's full of flavonoids and antioxidants and it's just the thing for a killer hangover." Actually, it was just the thing for keeping Mary from aging rapidly and drastically as a result of the resurrection she'd performed. "A little rosemary for the brain, valerian for the nerves, ginseng for strength, ginko for the circulation, garlic for the heart ...."

... and a little consecrated silver to fortify my spiritual strength, ground oak leaf to center my soul, and dried blood from my mother to preserve my flesh, she finished to herself.

Mary set the half-eaten bread aside and laid her head on the cool wood table. Her skull felt like it was filled with sloshing quicksand. God. She'd really pushed it this time. She'd done a rejuvenation on her husband only two weeks ago—she had no business doing a full resurrection so soon afterward.

But what else could she do? The longer she waited to raise Karl, the more decomposition set in, the bigger the risk he'd come out a twisted, soulless monster.

She worried about the effect her rejuvenations had on her husband. He'd been in his late sixties when they met and was recovering from a quadruple bypass. All the signs indicated he wasn't going to see the end of the decade. But he'd heard about her special services through a spiritualist he'd consulted for stock advice, and he offered her more cash than she'd seen before to cast a spell to add a few years back onto his life.

She'd done twelve rejuvenations on him in the four years since then. He'd recently celebrated his seventy-first birthday and looked a fit fortysomething. But with each rejuv she'd cast, he'd grown a little colder in manner and mind. He still smiled, still laughed, still took care in his foreplay with her, but when she looked in his eyes, she sometimes felt she was staring out into the cold blackness between the stars. Once upon a time, she was sure she'd seen something like love in those dark eyes of his. Now she wondered if it hadn't been a figment of her imagination, if she'd never really been anything more than a favorite investment to him.

Or maybe she'd stopped letting herself see anything but his natural coldness to justify her affair with Karl.

Yolanda set a glass of fresh juice on the table beside Mary's head.

"Now, don't you fall asleep before I get breakfast ready," Yolanda admonished.

"Don't worry, I'm awake." With effort, Mary sat up and took a sip of her juice.

Mary admired the graceful curve of Yolanda's neck as the younger woman turned back to the fridge. They'd been friendly enough the past four years, but weren't really friends. Mary had held Yolanda at arm's length because she felt she had to keep too many secrets to cultivate a real friendship with her. Maybe that had been a mistake.

"William hired you right out of high school, so you've been his housekeeper for, what, ten years now?" asked Mary.

Yolanda nodded as she cracked two eggs into the hot skillet. "Yes, about ten years."

"Did you two ever ...? You know. Get involved."

Yolanda gave her a sharp look. "What kind of girl do you think I am?"

"A young and pretty one. And don't tell me he's too proper to sleep with his employees, because I'm still on the payroll." She paused. "Look, I'm not going to get mad; I'm just asking."

Yolanda sighed, staring down at the coagulating eggs.

"I was nineteen," she said quietly. "I couldn't say no to him. I didn't *want* to say no. I dreamed that he might fall in love, and make me his wife. But it was just sex to him, and he lost interest after a few weeks. Afterward, I felt like I'd been his whore, and thought about quitting ... but jobs that pay this well aren't easy to find. Not for girls like me, anyway. So I stayed."

Yolanda gave her a quick, worried glance. "He hasn't tried to touch me since he brought you here, if that's what you thought."

Mary shook her head. "No, it's not that. I just wondered how well you knew him. Sometimes I don't think I know him at all."

"Why do you say that?" Yolanda turned the eggs and put two pieces of sausage in a separate pan.

"Yolanda ... do you think he loves me?" Mary asked.

"He *ought* to love you, after all you've done for him."

"I haven't done that much. I'm just a nurse." The savory smell of the frying sausage made her mouth water.

"Mary, I have *eyes*. I've seen the change in him. He was an old, sick man, and now he's back in the prime of his life."

"But do you think he loves me?"

Yolanda spoke carefully. "I think men like him know how to possess things and take care of things. They don't know how to love as women need to be loved."

Mary quietly sipped her juice while Yolanda grated sharp cheddar onto the eggs.

"Speaking theoretically," Mary finally said, "how angry do you think he'd be if I took a lover?"

"He'd be furious. Mr. Barrington doesn't like to share." Yolanda brought the steaming breakfast plate to Mary.

"Oh, this looks yummy, you're a lifesaver!" Mary picked up her knife and fork and started digging in.

"Mary ... you've been going out an awful lot. Mr. Barrington might not have noticed yet, but ... just please be careful. I would miss you if you were gone."

The phone rang.

"If that's William, please tell him I'm asleep," Mary said.

Yolanda hurried over to the phone in the corner.

"Yes? Oh, hello, Mr. Barrington," Yolanda said. "Is everything okay? Yes. She's still asleep upstairs. Tonight? Yes, I'll tell her. Are you sure everything is okay? Fine. Goodbye."

Yolanda hung up and walked back to the table. "Mr. Barrington wants to talk to you about something. He'll call back at 10, and he wanted me to make sure you'll be here."

"I'm not going anywhere." Even if she had the energy to go out, she wasn't about to leave Karl by himself. "I wonder what he wants?"

Mary speared another piece of sausage. Mid-lift, her hand began to shake, and the hairs rose on the back of her neck and arms. Her heart began to pound, faster and faster.

"Are you okay?" Yolanda asked.

Mary's chest felt constricted; it was hard to breathe, and harder to talk. "I—I don't know—"

Suddenly, Mary was floating disembodied above Karl's bed in the upstairs bedroom. The walls and curtains were on fire, but the flames were the wrong color, deep red and purple and green. The air was filled with thick red smoke and the stench of black magic. Karl was coughing and weakly calling for help. He looked *old*, his face sunken. He almost looked like William. Through the smoke, she saw a corpse lying in a wide pool of blood beside the bed. Her horror deepened as she realized the body was *hers* ....

Mary came out of the vision and found that she'd fallen out of her chair and lay crumpled on the floor. Yolanda was beside her, trying to help her up, but her legs weren't cooperating.

"What's the matter? Should I call for a doctor?"

We're going to die, Mary tried to say, shaking her head, but the words wouldn't come. Her vision clouded, and everything went black.

Mary came to a few minutes later as Yolanda hoisted her onto the bed in the first floor guest suite.

"What—" Mary began, still disoriented.

"Shh, be still. I'm going to ... call you a doctor," Yolanda said between gasps, winded from the effort of carrying Mary down the hall.

"No, don't. Don't need a doctor. Just need to rest," Mary slurred. She couldn't keep her eyes open. "I'm fine ... just need a nap. Please don't let me sleep too long ...."

Mary was running up the stairs of the mansion. Her legs moved too slowly, as if the staircase were covered in a foot of sticky tar that was sucking her down. The air stank of brimstone. From Karl's bedroom, she could hear a low, slithery voice chanting in a language older than mankind. The sound chilled her to the core. Something terrible would happen to Karl if she didn't stop it.

Mary finally got to the second floor and ran to the bedroom. The door was ajar, and a deep red light glowed from within. She pushed inside. The red light flared bright, blinding her, and the serpentine voice rose to a roar—

"Mary!" Yolanda was shaking her. "Wake up!"

"Oh God!" Mary jerked fully awake, breathing hard.

"Shh, shh, it's okay, it's just a nightmare. Everything's okay," Yolanda soothed, laying a cool hand against Mary's forehead. "I heard you call out in your sleep, and I thought I should wake you."

"Thanks." Mary sat up. A pain like someone had shoved an icepick behind her eyes lanced through her skull.

"God, what time is it?" Mary asked, clutching her head.

"Nine p.m."

"Twelve hours?" Mary threw off the thin quilt. "That's your idea of not letting me sleep too long?"

She rolled out of bed and staggered into the adjoining guest bathroom, turned on the faucet and splashed cold water on her face.

Yolanda followed her into the bathroom. "I tried waking you earlier, but you wouldn't get up. I didn't want to push you."

Mary found a bottle of aspirin in the medicine cabinet, and gulped down four tablets along with a handful of water. Her nerves were still humming from the alarm his ward spell had set off. "You've got to get out of here. Something really bad's going to happen."

"Mary, what's going on?"

Mary shook her head. "I can't explain. There's no time."

She stepped back into the bedroom and stuck a hand in her pocket to find the key to Karl's bedroom. Her fingers found nothing but lint. She'd left the key in her dirty jeans upstairs.

"You didn't happen to bring the dirty clothes down to the laundry, did you?"

"I put them in the wash." Yolanda reached into the breast pocket of her apron and pulled out the key. "Are you looking for this?"

"Yes."

Mary reached for the key. Yolanda dropped it back in her pocket.

"No. Not until you explain," Yolanda said. "*I* am responsible for this house when Mr. Barrington is away, and if there's a danger here, I need to know exactly what it is. 'Something bad' isn't a good explanation."

"Dammit, I can't—"

"When I was upstairs, I heard a noise in the second-floor bedroom. I was surprised the door was locked, but not half as surprised as when I found a strange man in there." Yolanda paused. "The blood on your shirt wasn't from a deer, was it?"

Mary took a deep breath. "No. It's wasn't. The man in the bedroom is … my boyfriend Karl. He wrecked his bike, and I brought him here."

"That boyfriend of yours is a real cutie. But he has an awful lot of stitches in him. I'm no doctor, but I think I can tell when a guy's had his head sewn back on. So how come your boyfriend is still breathing when he should be in a morgue?"

"I'm … a healer. A white witch. That's why William hired me. I could keep him alive when the doctors couldn't."

Mary closed her eyes for a moment, trying to steady her nerves. "Last night, I had a vision that Karl had an accident. He was dead when I found him, so I brought him here to bring him back. Since then, I've had … bad premonitions. Something very evil is coming here, and I honestly don't know what it is. I *do* know that if we don't get out of here, it's going to kill me and Karl, and probably you, too."

Yolanda paused, looking skeptical. "Maybe all this is happening because you helped Karl cheat Death?"

"No. I've done resurrections before, and nothing like this happened. Besides, by that logic, the spells I cast on William should've brought evil down on us, too.

Heart failure is just as fatal as decapitation. Neither of the men in my life should be alive right now."

Yolanda stared at Mary. "I knew of a Santeria witch woman once. She claimed she did white magic, too, but there was a blood price for everything she did. There was a balance. If she cured a cold, a chicken or a lizard had to die. If she helped someone stay alive, someone else had to die."

"There has to be a balance, yes. You can't generate magic out of nothing. Healing requires a lot of spiritual energy, and the easy way to get it is to take it from another life. But my mother taught me a better way: I can generate the energy myself, if I stay fit and eat right and all that good stuff."

"So you don't kill people?"

"Not unless they're trying to kill *me*."

Yolanda considered this, then pulled the key out of her pocket and tossed it to Mary. "Let's get your boyfriend and get out of here. If something happens to the house ... well, that's why Mr. Barrington has insurance."

After checking on Karl and replacing his I.V. bag, the two women went up to Mary's bedroom. Mary quickly laced on her old hiking boots and threw a few changes of clothes and some toiletries into an overnight bag.

"We've got to be really careful with Karl." Mary shook her head. "He shouldn't be moved at all, but we have no choice. There's an old wheelchair up in the attic. We can use that to take him out to the car."

Mary left her bag on her dressing table and knelt down beside her bed. She reached under it and pulled out a battered steel case.

"First things first," Mary said. "We've got to be able to defend ourselves."

Mary undid the combination locks and opened the case. She pulled out a large revolver, flipped open the cylinder and checked the contents. Satisfied, she closed the cylinder and held the pistol out to Yolanda. "Here, take this. It's loaded with consecrated silver bullets half-jacketed in cold iron. Ammunition against most anything, dead or alive."

Yolanda stared at the gun as if it were a very large spider. "I have never fired a gun in my life."

"It's easy: just point the gun at the thing you want to kill and squeeze the trigger."

When Yolanda didn't reach for the gun, Mary said, "Look, you've *got* to take it. It's iron; I can't have it on me, or it'll screw up any spells I try to cast."

Yolanda reluctantly took the pistol and stuck it in one of the deep side pockets of her apron.

Mary lifted an ancient silver-bladed bronze dagger in a red leather sheath from the case. It was an Irish priest's scían, made sometime in the fourth century. She stuck the holy weapon in the waistband of her jeans under her pullover. "Please get the wheelchair, and I'll prep Karl for the trip."

Mary grabbed her overnight bag and hurried down the stairs. The aspirin had only blunted the pain in her head, and her stomach was growling unpleasantly. At least her overlong sleep had given her most of her energy back. Once they had Karl squared away at a motel someplace, she could order a pizza and cast a divination to figure out what the hell was causing her visions.

Her stomach growled again, loudly. God, she was so hungry! If she didn't get more food soon, she'd lose what little concentration she had left. Mary dropped her bag beside Karl's bedroom door on the second floor landing and headed down to the kitchen.

As she was hunting for a Powerbar in the pantry, the back door opened.

"Who's there?" she called, putting a hand on the hilt of her dagger.

"It's just me, dear." William Barrington stepped out of the darkened entry hall into the light from the kitchen. He looked alert and cheerful, despite his long flight. "I'd have called to let you know I was returning early, but that would have spoiled the surprise. Please meet Nala, my new nurse."

A tall, beautiful model in a tailored green suit stepped up beside William. Her silken auburn hair cascaded down over her shoulders, and her eyes—Mary blinked, and did a double-take.

The woman's lovely high cheeks, pouting lips and green eyes seemed *transparent*, and behind the beautiful mask of a face Mary could just barely see the visage of something ugly and gray, something with skin that writhed and eyes like molten lead.

"I met Nala in Mexico City a few months ago," William said. "I appreciate all you've done, but the fact is, it's not enough. Nala can give me eternal youth. I've got to say her magical skills are quite impressive. Did you know she can pull a man's guts out through his mouth, and keep him alive indefinitely? She can also make the dumb son-of-a-bitch who's been fucking my wife wreck his motorcycle. Neat, huh?"

Mary's stomach dropped as she remembered her visions.

"But you *can't* be young again and remain William Barrington, can you?" she said. "So you have to become someone else. I get it. You planned to have *her* magic Karl's bones and teeth to look like yours, then kill me and burn the place down."

Mary took a step toward him. "The police would find the skeletons and think we'd both died in a freak fire. And then you'd take over the identity of whoever inherits the estate and the insurance money."

She paused, trying to remember the latest rewrite of his will. "It's your nephew George, isn't it? You're gonna kill him and Rita. Damn you, those kids just got married."

"You're a sharp girl; I always liked that about you." William's expression didn't change.

Mary swallowed nervously, trying hard not to look at Nala. "You didn't have to do this. I could've made you young again, and arranged a new life for you—"

"Bullshit." His eyes gleamed with fury. "How am I supposed to trust you after you've cheated on me? Do you think I can't smell that bastard's stink on you?"

"The only stink you're smelling is coming from your new girlfriend. Christ, she's not even *human*! The only eternal life you're gonna get out of this is the one she's booked you in Hell."

He smiled thinly. "I doubt I'll die to see it anytime soon. So be sure to send me a postcard when you get there."

Out of the corner of her eye, Mary saw Yolanda creeping down the stairs with the gun in her hands.

"This is taking too long," Nala announced. She had a voice like a nest full of copperheads sliding through the strings of a bass violin. "I need to get on with the boyfriend's transformation if we're going to be finished by dawn."

"Right," William said. "Kill her."

Nala hissed and made a grasping gesture with her left had. Mary gasped as invisible claws raked her innards and closed around her heart. Her whole body began to shake. She tried to speak a protective charm, but her tongue was paralyzed. She could only emit a thin moan as the agony became unbearable—

Fire flashed from the muzzle of Yolanda's revolver. The twin Magnum booms were deafening. Two bullets exploded through Nala's belly, leaving behind raw, saucer-sized craters that oozed black ichor.

The spectral claws abruptly released Mary. Nala roared, enraged and in pain, and turned on Yolanda. The demoness raised her hands and made a sharp push in the air.

An invisible force slammed into Yolanda's chest. She was flung backward into the stairs. Mary heard the crack of bone against wood. Yolanda bounced forward and tumbled down to the ground floor like a rag doll.

Mary was already whispering an incantation as she drew the silver dagger. She tackled the demoness, pinning her arms to the tile floor.

"With the power of the Goddess I cast thee, foul creature, from this house and from this living plane!" Mary shouted.

She grabbed the shrieking demoness by the hair and carved into her neck until she felt the metal grinding against bone. She whispered the ancient Gaelic words of banishment into Nala's ear.

"*Immee gys Niurin!*" she finished with a shout.

Mary gave a hard yank, and heard a wet popping. She wrapped both arms beneath Nala's chin and yanked again, hard as she could. Nala's head tore free.

The decapitated demoness shuddered, then fell limp. Her flesh and bones smoked, collapsed and disintegrated as if her body had been little more than a shell of flash paper. In seconds, there was nothing left but a sulfurous stink and a film of ash on the floor and on Mary's jeans.

William was still standing there, dumbfounded. "What—what have you done?" he finally stammered. "I already gave up my soul. Oh God. What the fuck is going to happen to me now?"

Mary stood up. "You're going to Hell, asshole."

She slugged him in the jaw with everything she had left. He tumbled backward and fell flat on his back, unconscious.

Mary looked around. Yolanda lay in an unmoving heap at the bottom of the staircase. Mary's stomach sank. She hurried to the housekeeper's side and gently rolled her over. Her neck was broken, and her eyes stared out at nothing. Mary couldn't find a pulse.

Tears welled in her eyes. "Goddammit, I don't have anything left. I can't help her. Unless ...."

Mary stared at her husband.

"What I've given, I can take away."

She dragged him over to Yolanda's corpse, washed her hands, and began.

Three weeks later, the first snow of the winter fell. Mary finished her conversation with the coroner and hung up the phone. She cinched her thick terrycloth robe tighter, wiggled her feet back into her bunny slippers and padded into the library.

Yolanda and Karl were reading on a quilt they'd spread beside the roaring fireplace.

"Well, looks like you two are feeling better," Mary said.

"Yes, much better," Yolanda replied. "Was that the coroner?"

Mary nodded.

"What did he say?"

"That Mr. William Barrington the Third died of natural causes: arteriosclerosis and coronary failure due to a long life of smoking and drinking and being a general heartless prick. The police are no longer interested in anything that may or may not have happened here last month. And so William's estate will officially become mine once the paperwork is sorted out."

"So what happens now?" Karl asked.

Mary sat down beside him and gave him a playful pinch. "What happens now is that *you* are going to give me a foot rub. A very *long* foot rub, because I am *beat*."

She lay back on the quilt and closed her eyes. "But please, be gentle. I'm in mourning."

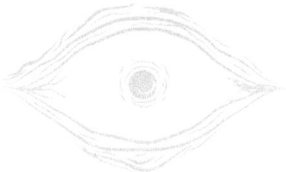

I Fuck Your Sunshine

Vampires? Of course I know them. You are surprised? Some call me ... what is it? "Fang hag." Ugh. Demeaning. I am crow to their wolves, eagle to their lions. You do not understand? I am succubus; the upyr and I, we do not compete, because we do not want the same thing. Sometimes, we feed on each other, yes: cock is cock, and blood is blood. Their seed is ... an acquired taste. Sour and bitter like rust, and sometimes it sticks in your throat like stale gummy candy. Not so zingy as live semen. But it takes the edge off!

I have known the Baron Stierherzov since before he turned to the night. He was a warrior lord, fierce in battle, merciless to the peoples he vanquished in the Old Country. Dracula himself gave him the eternal kiss as reward. Such a pedigree you do not find! I knew him when he was just a young boy eager for my visits. So full of delicious salty life! I could milk him over and over until his testicles bled, and still he would rise to please me.

So, it is only fair that I let him take my neck sometimes, now that we are equals. It is only necessary when he cannot hunt, after all; if he is housebound, then likely so am I. I miss the olden days of the plagues; you could take anyone you wanted, and unless someone glimpsed you winging away into darkness, who was the wiser? But now, every alleyway corpse is put under a microscope, put in the newspapers. So the Baron adapted, tries to live "green" as they say, and only takes a little here and there. It is frustrating to him, I know. And accidents happen, and then we all must stop feeding for a while.

The sun? No, of course it won't harm me. But it is not my ally, either. My glamour cannot hold under full light; there is not enough Estée Lauder in the world to fully conceal the 600 years in my skin. Oh, that is so kind of you to say, darling! But really ... for best hunting, the Baron and I need the same thing: darkness, and drunkards.

So, it was rotten luck for us all when Dansky's was torn down. Some conglomerate bought the whole block for a stupid mall, and they put an enormous Starbucks where the bar had been, can you believe it? Not so much as a drop of vodka to be found, so goodbye to all our drunkards. And all those dreadful windows and skylights! So much sun, and so many reflections—I made do, as a lady must, but poor Baron could not stand it, even after sundown.

There was only one reliable hunting ground left to him in the whole city: the Iron Pit Athletic Club. Open all night long, and no windows. He went in one evening, and I did not see him again for a whole nine months.

But when I did ... oh, what a sight he was.

It was noon; the sun burned high in the sky. Miserable cloudless day. But I sat there in the coffee house with my black tea, watching the people come and go. I had just spotted young man, shy, ordering a mocha latte, and I could smell the miasma of stifled lust on him. I stood up to go work my wiles on him when it happened.

"I FUCK YOUR SUNSHINE!"

It was an inhuman shout, loud as a war cannon. We all turned toward the noise, turned to stare out at the street, and I saw an absolute monster out there. A man-shaped thing, hulking, massive, muscle piled upon muscle, flesh wormed with thick veins. It strode down the street, naked, skin aflame in the relentless sunlight.

"I FUCK YOUR SUNSHINE!" the thing bellowed again. The purple flames devouring its flesh were rising higher and higher, skin blackening, curling like paper and ashing away, revealing gray-red muscle and yellow tendons beneath.

"I FUCK YOUR SUNSHINE!"

I recognized the voice ... it was the Baron! In an instant, I realized that for those nine months he'd been hiding behind concrete walls, he'd been lifting weights and drinking blood from the thick, brutish necks of hundreds of sweaty steroid junkies. His diet had made him huge, and the unnatural chemicals had inflamed his frustrations with the modern world until it drove him mad as a Spanish arena bull.

His eyeballs were burning in his skull like furnace coals as he strode up to the Starbucks; the glass in the door shattered from the heat of his burning flesh. The smoke pouring off him smelled like the corpse pyres of the old battlefields.

"I FUCK YOUR SUNSHINE!" he roared at all the suburbanites shrieking and scrambling to get away from him.

He stood there amid the chaos, burning in the sunlight streaming down from those hateful skylights, proud as he had ever been as the victor of countless duels, and my cold heart broke at the dire beauty of him.

He took another deep breath to bellow his war cry, and I heard a loud *pop!*

And he exploded, shattering all the windows, piercing the fleeing humans with the flaming shrapnel of his bones. Cutting glass rained down on me, slicing my flesh to ribbons, but I did not care—I could see his heart there in the wreckage of his blown-apart body. It glowed and smoked, but still it pulsed with power.

So I snatched it up and hid it beneath my blood-soaked blouse. I carried it to the safety of my dark apartment, and kept it beating in a jar of my own blood. Later, when I realized what I must do, I broke into the morgue at night and pulled the bits of his bones from the bodies of the dead. It was not much, but it was a start.

What? You do not understand? Come down the hall with me to the guest bath … come see.

There. Do you see how the blood moves in the middle of the tub? That's the throbbing of his heart. Already you can see his skull growing back together, and the tendons of his ribs. I am sure the organs and muscles should be next, and then his skin.

Oh, darling … no. Don't struggle. It is already done, see? You'll just waste your own blood. Let it flow. The Baron needs fresh every day, now. Soon he shall be awake, and he and I will hide no more. We shall treat this city and its people the way we should have treated them all along. We will be crow and wolf, eagle and lion.

We will fuck everybody's sunshine.

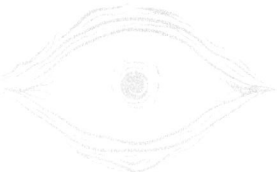

Carnal Harvest

Tonight was the night.

Gordon felt an electric tingle in his chest and belly. His cock had been awake since morning, rising and twitching like a hungry fish every time he thought of Judy McLarren. He'd sped to work that morning, cursing the Friday-morning traffic, and had attacked the pile of writs and briefs in his office with savage disdain until, at last, he'd shoveled the papery snowfall away like a good little junior partner and could leave the office early without raising too many eyebrows.

He'd been rock-hard when he stalked out of the office, and it had given him an extra measure of pleasure that the old dried-up clockwatching prune of a secretary on the first floor had noticed his condition, her eyes widening. When he'd smiled and winked at her, she'd blanched, her hand twitching upward as if she wanted to cross herself.

Gordon chuckled to himself as he toweled off his hair and stepped out of the bathroom. Oh, how he wished he could show that old crone exactly how much fun he was going to be having that evening. If a simple hard-on got her goat, he could only imagine the priceless look she'd wear if she could see what he had planned for sweet Judy. She'd piss her lavender polyester slacks and keel right over in a dead faint. Perhaps someday ... no. He shook his head. Why bother with a prune when there were so many cherries left to pick?

He carefully hung his towel on the drying rack by the radiator and stepped naked into his living room. The cool air felt good on his naked skin. His erection bobbed before him like a divining rod.

"Hungry boy," he cooed at it. "But you've got to cool it, or else you'll scare poor Judy. She'll take one look at you and know you'll burn her like the fire that made her a new virgin."

All Gordon's girls were new virgins: women who had been scarred so badly that they no longer had the company of men. Sometimes, the scars were physical, and men simply passed them over in favor of unblemished flesh. Often, the scars were in the women's heads—they thought themselves too ugly to have a man, or they had grown too afraid of love's agonies and kept themselves locked away. But Gordon knew that scarred fruit was still beautiful and luscious. And the challenge of wooing such women made them even sweeter.

He paused at the wet bar to pour himself three fingers of cherry kirsch. He swirled the clear liquor in his glass, then breathed in the heady aroma appreciatively. Judy was a real challenge. He still didn't know much about the fire that had killed her husband and turned the skin of her left hand and arm into a crepe-delicate lacework of scars. But he did know that she had no family or friends to care for her or check up on her; she'd almost completely withdrawn from the world. Even her job as a night auditor at a small hotel preserved her isolation.

But ever since the afternoon he spotted her at the grocery store, he had pursued her gently. First with flowers and love notes, then phone calls, then Sunday brunches after she got off work. And slowly, he had drawn her out of her shell. Tonight was their first true formal date. She'd taken a night off to be with him, and he would complete his seduction. She would tell him her secrets and open herself to him, body and soul. Tonight, Judy would be his and his alone. His to pluck and enjoy.

Still swirling his drink, Gordon walked to his trophy case and unlocked the black steel doors. He ran his fingertips over the smooth glass jelly jars inside. Each bore a carefully-penned label bearing his girl's names and the dates of their harvest.

"Ah, ladies," Gordon whispered. "Did you miss me? You'll have a new sister to keep you company after tonight. She's a beauty, and I'm going to enjoy her a great deal."

He lifted the first jar and held it up to the light, admiring the severed clitoris, inner labia, and nipples bobbing in the plum eau de vie within. "Sweet Belinda. You had the prettiest cunt. And your nipples were the most perfect pink. No one else ever imagined you had them, not with that face of yours." He slowly twirled the jar in the light, smiling as he remembered his date with Belinda. A neighbor's dog had attacked her when she was three, and had gnawed off her ear and most of her right cheek. Her family had been too poor for plastic surgery. Most people could scarcely look at her, but she had the kind of curves most women could only dream about. He'd been the happy recipient of years of pent-up sexual energy.

She was a real virgin, and she couldn't seem to get enough of his cock. He'd had her screaming even before he brought out his harvesting tools. "Judy has your coloring. I wonder if her tits are as pink and perfect as yours? Pity your flesh has grown so pale and gray over the years."

He put Belinda's jar back on the shelf and glanced at the clock on the wall. He was supposed to meet Judy at the Tremont Cinema in forty minutes.

"Sorry, ladies, I've got to run." He opened the drawer beneath the display cabinet and began to sort through his tools.

"Who wants to come with me tonight?" he asked the denizens of the drawer. He selected a roll of duct tape, his skinning knife, scalpel, dental forceps, chloroform bottle, and a fresh coil of nylon rope.

"Now, behave yourselves tonight," he said as he wrapped the tools up in a piece of plastic tarp. "We mustn't scare the girl before the time is right."

He blew the jars a kiss as he closed up the cabinet. "Be ready to welcome Judy when I get back."

The Tremont was in the Old City, nestled in the quaint little maze of shops and restaurants at the base of the hills of Memorial Park. The 200-acre city cemetery took up most of the park; some of the graves in the inner cemetery dated back to the late 1700s. As a boy, he'd enjoyed wandering amongst the old headstones, looking for the graves of women who'd died young. He liked to imagine how they had met death. As he got older, he liked to imagine that he was the one who had killed them.

Judy was waiting for him outside the theater. Her honey-blond hair was done up in a tidy French braid. She was wearing a flowered- print dress, pink silk cardigan, and Birkenstock sandals.

He smiled. She'd be able to walk in those sandals; that would make things easier. Of course, it had been most convenient that she had suggested the Tremont in the first place. With the deserted park nearby, he'd be able to enjoy her in the woods at his leisure.

As he approached her, he pulled a tissue-papered bouquet of a half-dozen red roses out of his leather shoulder bag.

"You look lovely," he said, presenting the roses to her with a gallant flourish.

Judy giggled nervously and ducked her head. "Oh, wow, you didn't have to … but they're great. I love roses." She took the bouquet, gave the roses a sniff, then stood there, crinkling his gift to her breast and rocking back and forth on her heels like a shy little girl.

She smiled at him, showing white, straight teeth. Her teeth really were quite good; should he collect them when he was done? Or perhaps her ears? Her ears curved delicately, perfectly; he didn't think he'd ever seen a better pair on a woman. Certainly not on Belinda. She had so many excellent features, and he hadn't even seen what she kept hidden under her clothes. It would be very hard to choose. He might have to find an extra-large jar for Judy.

"I … I was thinking maybe we could see that new Ryan Gosling movie?" she said. "But maybe that's too much of a chick flick for you. That new thriller is playing here, we could see it, instead, if you want?"

"Whichever you'd like is fine," he replied. "It doesn't matter what we watch, as long as I can see it with you beside me."

She decided on the romantic comedy. He paid for their tickets, and they walked into the darkened theater and settled themselves in seats on the back row.

Gordon scarcely paid any attention to the trifling film. His tools, which he'd carefully stowed in the bottom of his shoulder bag, were whispering to him, begging him to use them. Their voices were low and slithery.

He poked the bag sharply with his foot. "Shut up. You'll scare her away," he muttered at them.

The voices died down to a low, electric hum.

"Did you say something?" Judy asked.

"No, nothing. Just stubbed my toe."

A few minutes later, during a particularly romantic scene, he reached over and took her hand. She seemed surprised at first, but then her fingers laced into his and she relaxed.

By the time the movie was ending, she'd snuggled up close to him and was resting her head on his shoulder.

Hook and line, he thought. *Now I need to find a place to sink her.*

"Did you enjoy it?" he asked as they stepped out of the theater.

"Oh, yes," she replied, taking his hand again and tucking the bouquet under her arm. "It was wonderful. The ending was just dreamy. Thanks for inviting me; I'd have never gone to see it on my own."

"The pleasure is all mine," he replied.

The tools were hot in his bag, and they burned uncomfortably against his ribs. It annoyed him that they were being so impatient. *He* was in charge here. They'd have to wait for him to decide when the time was right. It wasn't just a matter of taking her body, after all; true seduction was all in the brain. Only when she'd told him the secrets of her soul would he know how he should harvest her.

"Would you like to get some coffee or dessert?" he asked her.

"Could we go for a walk, instead?" she asked uncertainly. "It's such a nice night, and the park will be pretty in the moonlight."

"A splendid idea," he agreed, trying not to smile too eagerly. The tools flared painfully.

"You've been so nice to me," she said as they walked hand-in-hand under the wrought iron archway that marked the entrance to the park. "I mean, you're a real gentleman. Not like most of the men I've known. Ever since the fire ..." she trailed off, staring into the distance. Then she shook herself from her reverie and smiled at him sadly. "It's just ever since then, I think I've had bad karma. I didn't seem to attract nice guys anymore, so I sort of stopped looking. And then you came along."

"Well, you're a very special woman to me. I think we were meant to meet."

He stopped on the path and pulled her close to him. "Would it be all right if I kissed you?"

She stared up at him, and her face darkened in horrified recognition. Her smile faded, and her eyes started to fill with tears. "Oh no ..."

He mentally cursed himself. Too much, too soon. "Shh, shh, it's all right, what's the matter?" he asked, fishing a handkerchief out of the side pocket of his shoulder bag.

She took the hanky, but pulled away, turning her back to him as she wiped at the tears. "I'm sorry. It's just, in this light, you look so much like him. Like my John. You've got his eyes."

"John was your husband?"

She nodded, sobbing quietly. "True love never dies, you know."

She took a ragged breath, then straightened up and faced him. "Have you ever been in love, Gordon?"

"Yes," he lied.

"What would you do for the one you loved?" she asked, her expression unreadable.

"Why, I'd move the sun and the stars to be with her," he replied smoothly. "I'd make sure nothing stood in the way of our love. I'd do anything I had to do to keep her by my side. Anything."

Judy took another deep breath, and her sad smile returned.

"My ... my John is buried over there, in the mausoleum," she said, pointing toward the cemetery. "I know this seems weird, but ... I just miss him so much, Gordon. Would you mind if we walked to his grave? I'd like to put one of these on his marker."

She touched the rose bouquet.

"It's not very far from here," she added.

Gordon's tools hummed. They liked the idea of the mausoleum. To fuck the girl on the cold marble floor, to harvest her in front of the sleeping dead … oh, that *would* be sweet.

"Certainly. If it would make you feel better, I'll be glad to go there with you," he said.

They walked in silence for a few minutes before he asked, "How did it happen? The fire, I mean."

When she didn't reply, he quickly added, "We don't have to talk about it if you don't want to—"

"No. No, it's okay. I don't mind talking about it. You have a right to know, since … since we're going to his grave and all." She gave him a quick, almost guilty smile.

Her teeth, Gordon thought. *I definitely have to take her teeth. And maybe her lips, too. Such pretty lips.*

"John was an anthropologist. He taught at the university before the fire. He specialized in comparative Afro-Carribean religions, and wrote a book about Santeria. He and one of the local Haitian priests he'd interviewed for the book, Hector Tambo, got to be really good friends. After John and I got married at St. Pete's, Hector suggested that he hold a private ceremony for us so that our marriage could be sanctified in the eyes of Olorun and the orishas, the spirits that watch over us. It sounded like a neat idea to me, so after we got back from our honeymoon, the three of us gathered at Hector's house for the ceremony."

Judy paused, frowning. "I still don't really remember what happened next. We were just starting the ritual when there was this incredible explosion. I woke up on the front lawn, surrounded by paramedics. Half the neighborhood was on fire. They said there was a gas leak in the basement, and when Hector lit some incense, most of the gas main ignited. John and Hector were dead. They said I was lucky to be alive."

She shook her head. "But I wasn't lucky. Not at all. When a ceremony like that goes unfinished, when true lovers are separated like that, the orishas take matters into their own hands."

They passed under some cherry trees and walked up the path to the mausoleum, broadly square and gray in the moonlight. Wrought iron lamps with weak yellow bulbs lit the entrance and interior walkway. Gordon's tools were humming louder and louder, and his cock was straining against his underwear.

Very soon, he thought. *You'll have her very soon.*

She took his hand and led him into the mausoleum.

"I didn't really think I'd take you here," she said sadly. "I mean, you're such a nice guy. This isn't the place for you. I wish the orishas had brought me someone else. But I can't help it. True love never dies, and you've got his eyes."

There came the low rumble and scrape of stone sliding against stone, then a booming slam as a section of marble hit the floor. Startled, he stared toward the noises. One of the grave drawers was open. And something large and black was crawling out.

Gordon's tools went silent, frigid. Judy gripped his wrist tightly, painfully. He tried to pull back, but she held him fast.

"John, I've brought you a visitor," she called.

The black thing shambled up to them with alarming speed. It was the burned, skeletal corpse of a big man, well over six feet tall. Its charred tissues had been stitched over in a green-gray patchwork of newer dead flesh.

The thing leered down at him with its empty black eye sockets. The stench from it was unspeakable. Gordon wanted to scream, wanted to throw up, but nothing came out of his throat.

The thing picked Gordon up and slammed him against the marble wall, holding him there fast, his feet dangling helplessly.

Judy stepped up beside them and caressed the thing's arm. "True love," she sighed. "John loves me, and I love him, and we'll do what we must to make love tonight. The orishas have made this our blessing and our curse."

She carefully set down the rose bouquet and opened up her purse. She pulled out a stainless steel pocketknife, a surgical needle and spool of suture. "We'll be needing your skin, and your lips and tongue. And of course your dick."

Gordon tried to kick at the thing, and found that his strength had evaporated like alcohol on a hot iron.

"But first things first." Judy reached up and gently pulled up his left eyelid. The knife flicked open in her hand, the blade gleaming silvery sharp. "You've got his eyes …."

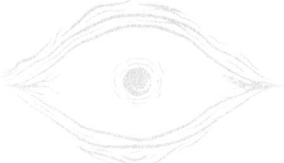

Antumbra

I woke in the afternoon gloom to the sound of my 20-year-old stepsister Lily dragging something heavy and wet up the back patio steps through the kitchen door. The smell of blood and brine smothered me the moment I sat up.

I swore to myself and called down to her: "What did you do?"

"You'll see," she sing-songed.

"Pleasant mother pheasant plucker." I lay back on the sweat-stained sheets for a moment to gather my focus. Four hours of sleep wasn't enough to keep my head from spinning, but it was all I could seem to get these days. The cells in my body kept waiting for the moon to move, despite all my meditating to try to tell them that the big rock blotting the sun wasn't going anywhere.

I kept having nightmares from everything I saw in the months after the Coronado Event. In the worst dream, I was sitting in my bedroom when an earthquake hit. The walls would crack, revealing not drywall and wood but rotten meat, and cold blood would pour in, flooding everything. The red tide would sweep me off my bed and press me up against the ceiling. My stuffed toys turned into real animal carcasses floating by my head. I'd be struggling to breathe in the two inches of air between the gore and the plaster when I felt something grab my ankle. And then I'd wake up.

I was a high school senior when it all happened. Back then I was so focused on prom and graduation and other such bullshit that I didn't notice the first reports on CNN that an astronomer named Gabriel Coronado had spotted a large, dark object hurtling toward the earth at barely sublight speeds. But the science geeks at my school started talking about it, so the rest of us finally paid attention. Some of the religious kids said it was going to be the end of the world. But everyone else figured it would be like one of those big-budget movies where they send a heroic team of astronauts up with good old American nukes to blow the comet/asteroid to smithereens before it reaches the Earth.

I think NASA and the Pentagon tried to pull some kind of mission together. Or at least that's what they told the media to try to calm people down. Their astrophysicists told them the big black object out there was going pass by, so they probably figured they just had to keep people from looting and committing mass suicide.

And it did miss us by half a million miles. But it was so huge and moving so fast it jerked the Earth and moon in its gravitational wake like a couple of hobos spun around in the wind from a speeding semi. When the storms and earthquakes and wildfires from meteor strikes passed, the Earth and moon were locked in a new static orbit.

Our city was in permanent lunar eclipse, which was far better than the relentless daylight some parts of the world suffered if you didn't consider the massive flooding we got from being stuck at high tide. The ocean invaded our city, and Cat 5 hurricanes blasted us every spring because of all the hot air blowing in from the lightside. But at least we weren't broiling.

After ten years of living in the antumbra, my body still hadn't adjusted to the new normal. All my cycles were screwed up. Sometimes I'd bleed twice in a month, and then half a year would pass before I kicked another egg. At least I had my life, which was more than about four billion people could say. And I mostly had my health, even if I was turning into a bona fide lunatic.

Lily, on the other hand, was thriving like apocalypse was that special vitamin she'd been missing as a kid.

"Are you sleeping, are you sleeping, sister June? Sister June?" she sang off-key from the kitchen. "I got something for you, I got something for you, yum yum food! Yum yum food!"

"Okay, okay, I'm coming." I crawled off the bed, pulled on a tee shirt, and stumbled downstairs.

Lily stood peacock-proud in gore-soaked clothes beside a massive hunk of *something* that she'd dragged in on a sled of black trash bags and flattened cardboard. The coppery smell of blood and the bay stink made my eyes water. It was cylindrical, maybe four feet long and two feet in diameter. I didn't see any bones in the ruby-red flesh. The black skin of the thing was covered in fur, like that of a seal or otter, except for where it had a double row of naked purple suckers as big as saucers.

"Where did you get this?" I asked her, frowning down at the massive hunk of tentacle.

"It didn't come from a people!" Lily exclaimed, as if that was the alpha and omega of all my possible questions. "Will you cook it? It's all bitter raw."

"I'm glad it wasn't a person." We'd had a long talk when she was nine about how it was wrong to eat people. I'd mostly done it to convince her to stop biting neighborhood kids she didn't like. Later, she saw a TV show about dolphins and decided that anything that could communicate was a person. Cats and dogs became people to her, and that was just as well. She got hungry for meat and bones a whole lot during her growth spurts and I couldn't watch her all the time. "But where did you get it?"

"It came up from the sea." She shrugged. "Hungry. Tried to eat people. I helped the Robichaud guys kill it."

I frowned at her. "And what were you doing with the Robichaud brothers?"

Lily crossed her sinewy arms behind her and rocked side to side like a guilty preschooler. She licked her lips with her impossibly long tongue, running it briefly over her chin. "Just helping."

"Helping" my ass. Christ. Well, at least I'd gotten Doc Freeman to give her an IUD. I stared down at the tentacle. The doctor would give us good trade for organs from a creature like this. I didn't know what the hell she did with them, but apparently monster parts were useful to someone's research somewhere.

"It's a shame you only got this," I said. "Doc Freeman would have liked more."

"I got more!" Lily smiled, her sharp teeth gleaming in the fluorescent light, and pointed behind me. "In there. An eye and a brain-thing. In ice, like she said."

I followed her point to the dining room table, and saw a stained Styrofoam picnic cooler that had been duct-taped shut. "Oh. Sick. Good job, sis."

The tentacle passed muster with the food safety scanner; it was a little radioactive, but so was every damn thing since the Coronado Event. The planet got hit with about a billion space rocks following in the big black's wake, and they were loaded with uranium and God knew what. Maybe some of the rocks came from planets the big black smashed, worlds that had their own strange forms of life. That would explain a whole lot about what was happening to the Earth.

Doc Freeman had given us the scanner in exchange for a crate of scotch we salvaged from a drowned mansion. It had saved us from being poisoned probably a dozen times. Well, saved *me*, anyhow; nothing ever seemed to make Lily sick these days.

She helped me cut the tentacle into thick steaks. I wrapped half and put them in the freezer, threw two on our electric grill, and put the rest in the fridge. Thanks to good loot trades, we were pretty well fixed for hydrogen fuel cells, so we didn't have to be too stingy with electricity. I could deal with all the humidity and mildew that came with giving up our air conditioning for the sake of the grow lights for our indoor herb garden, but the thought of drinking warm beer was just too much to bear.

The mystery meat grilled up nice and tender with some wine, soy sauce and what was left of our scallions; if I closed my eyes I could pretend it was a filet mignon. But my memory of what beef really tasted like was hazy. The light from the corona around the moon screwed up my sleep, but it wasn't enough to grow grass for cattle. We had to get corn and wheat from penumbra states like Nebraska, if we could get them at all.

"Watermelon." Lily was gazing mournfully at her clean-licked plate. "I want watermelon."

"Maybe soon," I said. "Doc said the caravan should be back in a month or two."

She stared down at her blood-crusted nails. "Dirty. I should wash?"

"Yes, you should."

Lily gazed at me with her big orchid-purple eyes, looking every bit the changeling my stepfather claimed she was the day he walked out our door and stole my Mustang. I'd worked three summers straight to save up for that car. I borrowed a boyfriend's van and ran after the bastard to get my property back, make him take responsibility for his daughter for just once in his lousy life. But he got himself killed trying to steal fuel before I could catch up to him.

My mom had already died in the epidemic after the meteorite storm; before her throat closed up, she'd made me promise to look after Lily. She probably knew her dad would bail on us sooner or later. I was fifteen when they met, and I knew right away what she saw in him. Dude needed an inseam zipper. They married before anyone knew about the big black, of course; otherwise she'd have found a guy with survival skills. Mom was never dumb on purpose. But she was making good money selling real estate, so what else did she need a man for back then?

Lily was eight when I met her, and already full of bad habits from her dad's mix of spoiling and neglect. He was vague about who her mother was. I guess she must have been a hot mess for anyone to award custody to a slackerjack like him.

My stepsister never seemed exactly normal brain-wise, but she looked human enough when she was young. That all changed after her dad was gone. She got the same fever that killed my mom, but the worst it did was make her teeth fall out.

A new set grew in, almost reptilian, and needle-sharp. Her eyes changed, and she started getting muscles that made some people mistake her for a boy.

We met Doc Freeman when I took my sister to the city's free clinic to make sure she was okay. The doc took a real interest in Lily, and by extension me, and got us medicines and such when we needed them. I once asked the doc why she was fascinated with Lily, and she went off on this long lecture about virally induced mutations and epigenetics and evolution. I only understood some of what she was telling me, but the take-home was that Lily's blood might be useful for making vaccines or serums that the labs on the darkside were creating. The darksiders were making all the best stuff these days; they had to, or else they'd have nothing to trade with the countries that could still grow food.

"I need a shower." Lily licked her lips again, staring at me like I was something she wanted on her plate. "Shower with me."

Dread and anticipation coiled inside me. I knew what she wanted. And I knew I should say no. Touching her was wicked, but I'd been doing it for years. It started after we left my hometown to try to find a better place. For months it was just the two of us and miles of dark and cold and wet wreckage. We were both going crazy from fear and hormones, and when she crawled into my sleeping bag and kissed me that first time, it seemed like the best way to take care of her. That's what I told myself, anyhow.

We weren't alone in the world anymore … but it wasn't like the Robichaud boys ever wanted to spend any time with *me*. They and everybody else just had eyes for Lily. Sure, a couple of the other guys in the neighborhood regularly inquired after my swallowing abilities and generously offered me the use of their boners. But all that hot romance aside, they seemingly thought soap was just something you stuck in a sock to use as a weapon.

"Okay," I said. "Let's take a shower."

Ten minutes later, I had two fingers knuckle-deep inside her as the warm water beat down on us.

"Ah! There. Yes," she said, digging her nails into my shoulders.

I stroked her inside the way she liked … and realized something was missing. "I can't feel your cord."

"Pulled it," she gasped.

"What?" I took my hand away, horrified.

"Pulled it out." She frowned up at me, clearly annoyed that I was interrupting sexytimes with something so boring.

"Why?"

"Don't like it." She was starting to look as pissed off as I felt.

"You'll get pregnant without it!"

"So?" She crossed her arms over her breasts.

Rage surfing on thirteen years of frustration crested inside me. "So we can't have a fucking baby, are you stupid?"

It felt like I was having to explain one of the basics to her all over again: don't bite people, don't run with scissors, don't eat rotten meat.

Lily snarled and chomped me on the shoulder, hard. I hollered and shoved her off me. She hit her head on the moldy tile wall, cursed me and punched me in the stomach. I tumbled out of the tub, tearing the old vinyl shower curtain down with me, and landed in a heap on the hairy floor beside the toilet. Blood was spilling out of the bite wounds on my shoulder.

My stepsister stared down at me, looking scared and confused.

"Jesus." I sat up, shook off the dirty curtain and touched the skin around the bite to try to see how deep it went. It was the worst one she'd given me yet, and my flesh was already swelling up and turning purple. "You and your fucking spit venom. You really get on my last nerve sometimes, you know that?"

I got myself bandaged up with some tape and gauze pads. Lily hovered around asking if she could help, but I was too angry to do anything but tell her to sit on the couch downstairs and stay out of my way. I got dressed, grabbed the Styrofoam cooler, and hauled it over to Doc Freeman's office. Stabbing pains were shooting down my whole right arm by the time I got there and blood had soaked through the gauze into my tee shirt.

"Oh! That doesn't look good," the doctor said as she came out of the exam room. She was wearing a crisp white lab coat and freshly shined boots, as usual; I never could figure out how she always managed to look so put together and professional considering all the nasty stuff she had to handle. I was lucky to make it through a day of scavenging without getting a new hole in my clothes.

I could hear a faint motor whine as her artificial eye focused on me. The whole upper left of her face was cybernetic; the rumor was that she'd been hit with a pea-sized meteorite, a cosmic bullet to the skull, but her family was rich and got her to a reconstructive neuroengineer right away.

"It doesn't feel so good." I set the cooler down on the receptionist's desk.

"Lily?" Doc Freeman asked.

"Lily." I nodded.

"Well, let's take a look." She helped me take my shirt off and the sodden bandages nearly came with it. "Oh, she got you good, didn't she? What happened?"

"I found out she pulled out her IUD. I told her she can't have a baby. *We* can't."

"Oh, my." The doctor began to clean my wound with betadine. "You realize she *can*, though, right? She's allowed. She's an adult; it's her choice."

I craned my neck to stare back at her incredulously. "I cannot believe you're saying that. She's a fucking child. A *dangerous* child. You *know* that. She's got no business having a baby."

"You're worried you'd end up with child care duties?" Doc Freeman injected me with antibiotics, then followed it with a shot of the antivenin she'd made after the first time I reacted badly to one of Lily's bites. Making venom in her saliva glands was a fairly new trick; lucky for me the doc figured out what was going on right away.

"Of course I'm worried!" I replied. "Even assuming the baby took after the dad and not Lily, I couldn't handle her *and* her kid."

"Still. She's an adult. As are you. You can always leave her to fend for herself."

"No." I squeezed my hands into fists on my lap. "That's what her father did. I won't do that to her."

The doctor silently wrapped my shoulder in fresh gauze.

"Can you honestly look at me and tell me that you think that having a baby is in Lily's best interest?" I asked. "Medically, psychologically? Can you say that? And would it be any good for the baby? C'mon, look at me—this is how she deals with being told 'no.'"

The doctor sighed. "Much as it would be interesting to see the result of her pregnancy … no, I can't say it would be in her best interests."

"Can you help me out here?"

"What do you want me to do?" The doctor looked angry. "Sterilize her against her will?"

"No. I just … I just want to keep her out of trouble. Is that so wrong? I just want a little control here."

The doctor's expression was unreadable. "I can give you all the control you can take. But that, my dear, will cost you."

I gingerly slipped my bloody shirt back on. "I've got something in the cooler over there that might be worth it to you."

The doctor went to the Styrofoam container and cut the tape off with a pair of surgical scissors. I hopped off the exam table and followed her over, curious. She lifted the lid off and exposed a multi-pupilled gray eye the size of a cantaloupe and a brain that was twisted like a giant cruller.

Something dark passed over her features for just a fraction of a second, but then she smiled. "*Very* interesting. And where did these come from?"

"Something that crawled out of the sea today."

"Ah. I heard about that. I went to investigate but the carcass had already been thoroughly butchered."

She replaced the lid and went to the safe where she kept her most valuable bits of biotechnology. "Bear in mind that what I'm about to give you is not a medical device. It was developed for the military, and was not perfected. Do you understand?"

"As in, it might not work?"

"Yes."

"So what are the side effects?" I didn't ever worry that she was giving me something dangerous; my gut told me there was no way she would do anything that might hurt Lily. My stepsister was too important to her. But I didn't want to get sick if it wasn't even going to work.

"Not well documented, I'm afraid. Headaches, vertigo, confusion, and nausea are reported to be the big ones."

"What is it, this device?"

"Here." She handed me an unlabeled blister pack containing two gel capsules, one red and one clear. Each was filled with some kind of glittery fluid.

"These both contain synchronous cerebronanobots," she said. "The clear is for the controller, and red is for the target. Both the controller and the target take the capsules orally. Then, once the nanobots have entered the bloodstream and successfully crossed the blood-brain barrier, they take up residence in the frontal and temporal lobes. Once they've synched, the controller should begin to have empathic access to the target's mind and can, at least in theory, exercise some control. You replace your target's superego with your own, if you succeed."

"Wow." I uncertainly took the blister pack from her hand. "That's pretty heavy stuff."

"It is. But I expect she'd pull another IUD or cut out a subdermal implant. The only other option would be for you to bring her here for hormone shots every three months. I doubt she'd be very cooperative. The nanobots are all I have to offer you."

"You gave me some kind of new infection," I told Lily when I got back to the house.

"I sorry." Tears rolled down her cheeks. She always got extremely remorseful for a few days after she bit me.

"Doc Freeman gave us pills to take." I held up the blister pack.

She made a face. "Don't like pills."

"Well, I don't like them either. But we both have to take them."

I poured us two glasses of water and broke the capsules out of their blisters.

"Down the hatch." I handed her the red one.

"Why mine diff'rent?"

"Because the infection didn't make you sick." I'd thought my lies out carefully on the walk back to our house. "Because you're a carrier, and I'm not."

"Oh. Okay." She took the capsule from my hand and swallowed it down with a gulp of water.

After a quick, silent prayer to a god I no longer believed in, I swallowed mine down as well.

We settled down on the couch to watch her favorite cartoons, and she laid her head on my good shoulder. I waited to see what would happen. For the first hour, nothing was different. But then came a faint buzzy feeling in my head, an electric warmth, a melting sensation. I realized that I could feel how my own shoulder felt against her cheek.

Before I fully realized what was happening, she was in my lap, kissing me, pulling my jeans off. I couldn't even summon the clarity to wonder where my will had gone. We fucked for hours in the blue light of the television; in the morning, we ate bitterly raw steaks straight from the refrigerator and stumbled out, hand-in-hand, to go see the Robichaud boys.

Hours melted into days melted into weeks. It was all dreamtime for me, an erotic nightmare from which there was no waking.

I came back to myself, briefly, in a room in a flooded mansion. I was alone, sitting on a rotting red velvet couch beneath a chandelier dripping with algae, but I could hear Lily moaning in the room above me. I could feel the webbed claws clutching her, the strange appendages slithering into her as she writhed, and I tried to stand, to stop what was happening, but the orgasm took her and my mind went with it, down, down into the murky water.

I didn't surface again until months later in a flooded laboratory. I found myself blinking in a fluorescent glare, holding Adam Robichaud's blond head under the water; I'd already drowned him. Lily was up on what looked like a dentist's chair, naked, panting hard, her distended abdomen rippling. I realized my mind was no longer bound to hers, and the sudden absence filled me with cold loneliness. Doctor Freeman stood behind her, smoothing her hair away from her face, whispering encouragements to breathe.

Lily wailed as the baby began to squeeze through. First the head, then an arm that was jointed in too many places …

"Oh god," I whispered when I got a good look at the infant.

"Oh, June, excellent, you're back with us." Doc Freeman caught the baby as it slithered out, deftly keeping her hands clear of the snapping mouth. "I am afraid I told you to take the wrong capsule. I just couldn't have you interfering in my work any longer. But as you can see, everything has turned out well in your absence."

"What …?" I began.

"I made a people!" Lily grinned at me, glowing with maternal pride. She looked happier than I had ever seen her.

"Yes you did!" Doc Freeman smiled back at her. "And this little fellow is quite hungry. Keep breathing, my dear!"

The doctor sloshed past me and set the newborn down on Adam's floating corpse. The little creature latched onto his naked back with its sucker mouth and began to devour his flesh.

"Welcome to *Homo freeman*," the doctor said. "The first of his kind, and certainly not the last."

"Oh!" Lily gasped. Her belly rippled again.

"Three more to go!" the doctor called. "Keep breathing and pushing!"

I took a step toward them, and felt a sharp cramp and heavy pressure in my own belly. It was not a sympathy pain. Terror filled me as I looked down and saw my nine-month bump.

"Once your nephews are all born, I expect it'll be time to induce you, dear June. Your child will not be as exotic, I'm sure, but she'll come in handy just the same."

I turned and tried to flee, but my nephews' alien father rose up out of the water, looking like a cross between a frog god and the worst fever hallucination I'd ever had, and clutched me to its clammy torso.

"Save your strength," Doctor Freeman called. "Believe me, you'll be needing it soon enough …"

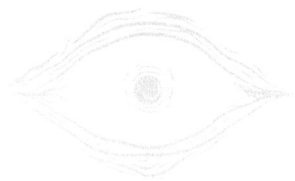

Diamante and Strass

The Queen of Montana stood regal before her icy throne as her guards hauled in the notorious man-eater Giorgia Diamante and her accomplice, Elvira Strass.

"Are these the gunslingers?" The Queen looked down her long, thin nose through her kaleidoscope monocle at the dusty duo.

"*She's* a gunslinger. I'm a bomber," said Strass.

Diamante gave her a sharp elbow in the ribs to shush her. The thickly furred floor beneath them twitched indolently and the zebra-striped walls breathed in afternoon slumber. The castle was far too familiar with the pheromones of murderers to be concerned about the girls.

"Yes, Mum, they are the ones you requested." The captain of the Queen's guard pulled a savage, snub-nosed machine pistol from beneath his sky-black cape. "We found this customized weapon on Miss Diamante's person."

"I call it the Dance." Diamante tipped her woven steel Stetson toward the Queen. "St. Vitus style."

"In the olden days," the queen observed with an arched eyebrow, "dancing was like exploding."

Diamante gave her a curt, knowing nod. "That piece'll give 'em all a decent overloading."

"It connects to something in your hip?" The Queen peered at Diamante's left side.

Diamante touched the lumpy scars on her tanned flesh above her low-slung leather ammo belt. "Neuromilitary implant. The Dance links to my optic lobe and fires in perfect synch with the diastole of my heart. I just have to *think* about it and the whole room's dead."

"What a soft bounce!" the Queen marveled.

"She's a hot machine." Strass impatiently pushed back her thick golden hair. "But surely you didn't bring us here to jawbone hardware. What can we do for your Majesty?"

The Queen pulled a digital wand from the folds of her shimmering robes and pointed it at the fuzzy floor in front of the duo. She flicked it on, and a bust hologram of a skinny man with a wild, dirty-blond mane and an equally unkempt beard spilling over a priest's collar appeared before them. The pupils of his blue eyes were mismatched: the right was as small as the point of a dagger and the left was as big and dark as a Stimjim tablet.

"Bring me the head of this preacher," the Queen ordered.

"That's Reverend Dr. Johnny Swarovski." Diamante squinted at the flickering holo of the thin white man. "He used to be your Duke, didn't he? Before he invented his secret formula."

The Queen acted as if Diamante hadn't spoken. "Johnny's an American, but he's fled across the border. My signet ring will guarantee his extradition should local knights intervene."

She slipped the signet off her pinkie finger and flipped it to Diamante. "The spy in my cab told me Johnny's holed up in the desert outside Medicine Hat with his … acolytes."

"Acolytes? How many?" Diamante frowned as she wiggled the ring into the tight front pocket of her jeans.

The Queen smiled at her. "Surely you're not afraid of Americans?"

Diamante frowned. "I'm not afraid of the world. What's in this deal for us?"

"A clean slate," the Queen replied. "We'll drop the bass, murder, cannibalism, corpse defilement, and public intoxication charges from the rave in Anaconda."

"Ezekiel," spat Strass. "That dirty jerk."

"He got what was coming. They *all* did." Diamante's eyes glittered. "You'd have done the same."

"Maybe I would." The Queen gave the daintiest of smiles and shrugs. "But do my bidding, and there shall be no cell block tangos for you girls in my domain. And of course there's more."

The Queen snapped her fingers, and two of her guards brought forth a bulletproof tortoiseshell case and popped the horny locks. In amongst the pulsing guts of the tortoise were dazzling pounds of glittering pale gems.

"My best friends, and soon yours," the Queen said. "Provided you bring me the good Reverend's head."

"Did you want the rest of him past his neck?" Strass asked.

"Not necessary." The Queen pursed her lips. "But I do want the head brought back intact. *Alive*. And … unmolested."

So Diamante and Strass kitted themselves out in the finest rhinestone body armor the queen's arsenal could supply, packed up their weapons and a good medical stasis unit, fueled their biogas Harleys and rode north up the ruins of I-15.

They stopped at the Coutts border crossing like regular citizens; this was the first time in years that they hadn't jumped the wall. The rest of the traffic was mostly cargo beasts, NAFTACorp assault dinosaurs, and a few hand-painted vans full of various doomsday cultists headed to the North Pole. It was a nervous half-hour wait; Diamante's hand kept straying toward the St. Vitus Dance, and Strass' fingered the lumpy outlines of the white phosphorous grenades she had stashed in her bra.

But the strolling Death Mounties in their humming red power armor gave neither the gunslinger nor the mad bombshell a second glance.

"Where you gals headed?" The border agent pressed his sizzling brand into the fleshy page of the gunslinger's passport. The booklet quivered and squeaked in his hand.

"Medicine Hat," Diamante replied.

"Oh, be careful out there." He gave her a smile that was two parts grandpa concern and one part raptor leer. "Take the northern route through Vauxhall; the highway through the Glassy Desert ain't safe."

"Why?" Strass handed over her own struggling passport.

"Why, there be monsters!" He branded a page, and her booklet urinated on his wrist; he didn't seem to notice. "Goths and rockabillies. Transpsychic bandits. And other creatures that ain't fit for Thor's clean earth!"

They passed the Taber Starship Impact Memorial and turned onto the highway that transected the endless shimmering craze of green glass like a dark laser burn. Suddenly, Diamante's motor began to rattle. Soon the whole Harley was shaking like a junkie. A few moments later, Strass' motorcycle started jerking, too.

They pulled off to the side of the highway. Diamante got out her flashlight and inspected their machines. Tiny blue silicon worms, hatched from eggs carried on the dusty winds, had invaded the engines. The wrigglers were devouring the metal, leaving behind sticky trails of epoxy; the cylinders were nearly clogged with the acidic purple goo.

"Damn shitburners!" Diamante kicked a tire. "I *knew* we should have sprung for ceramic Vincents!"

"Well, this ain't good." Strass shaded her eyes and squinted out across the glaring barrens. "This place is still full of radium … if we have to walk the rest of the way, our bones'll be glowing by the time we get there."

Overhead, they heard a tiny sonic boom. A rocket-powered swallow dove straight down from the sky and landed on a spar of broken glass. When the cyborg scissor-tail opened its beak, the Queen of Montana's voice came out, thin and sing-song.

"Don't dilly or dally," the Queen told them sternly. "I have word that the Duchess of Minneapolis wants Johnny dead. No head. She's sent her Raspberry Berets to jam him."

Diamante swore and kicked the tire again. The swallow gulped and rocketed away.

"Well, that's a fine kettle of cocks." Strass shaded her eyes again and resumed scanning the dazzling plain.

"We'll have to hitchhike," Diamante said. "We've got to get out of this place."

"I think I just spotted our rides," Strass replied. She dug her noise bomb kit out of her saddlebag, extracted the amplifier and set it up on the pavement. She plugged in her microphone and started beatboxing, hissing and spitting rhymes and grunts out at whatever she'd seen in the bright distance.

Diamante heard Strass' beats echoed back, faintly at first, but then louder and louder, the harmonics shifting and multiplying as dark shapes rose on the garish horizon and moved closer and closer.

Soon, the shimmering glass mirage cleared enough to reveal huge cybersonic lizards, each the size of a tour bus. All were the descendants of feral iguanas who'd been impregnated and mutated by eldritch technologies from the starship crash that glassed the desert. Each iridescent scale on their saurine bodies acted as a tiny speaker pounding back the sounds that Strass sent forth. The cybersonic lizards bobbed their heads and flicked their blue tongues in time with the beat.

The lizards circled Strass and Diamante, fascinated by the music, but unwilling to let themselves be touched.

"Let me try," whispered Diamante. She got into her own saddlebag and unfolded her air guitar, brushed her fingers through the virtual strings for a quick tune-up, and began to play "Purple Haze." Strass switched up her beat to back Diamante's music, and the lizards made the glass quake as they writhed in appreciation.

As Diamante hit the climax, one opalescent lizard was entirely overcome by her hot licks. He fell forward onto the pavement, scales buzzing and crackling with feedback, rolled over and offered his pink neck and belly to the girls. While Strass scratched the lizard under his massive chin and sang "Suffragette City" to keep him still, Diamante fashioned a halter and reins out of her spool of carbon fiber rope.

Once they harnessed the scaly beast, the girls climbed atop his ridged back and urged him up the highway. He lumbered slow and steady for miles, until the wind shifted and his scales began to vibrate in sympathy with a cacophony in the distance. They heard voices, yes, and music, but it was all too chaotic to be a concert, too profane to be religion, too apocalyptic to be just another party.

"Johnny?" asked Strass.

"Johnny," agreed Diamante. "Let's get our man."

The lizard slithered them from highway to hills, and around midnight they crept up to the edge of a vast, fog-filled amphitheatre that Swarovski's legion of acolytes had dug in the blood-black earth with their own hands. The stink of narcotic incense and alcohol and sweating flesh was nearly overpowering.

"It's like the bowl of the bong of the gods." Strass pulled her bandanna up over her nose and mouth.

The Reverend Dr. Swarovski stood in the center of the amphitheatre on a bare dirt stage, barefoot in a gold lamé robe, speaking in tongues into a microphone. He was ringed by his thousands upon thousands of dancing, ululating worshippers who were pounding away on improvised instruments: toxic waste barrel drums, AK-47s fashioned into electric basses, whistles made from sniper rifle cartridges. Only a few of his celebrants appeared to be human.

Swarovski waved a golden aspergillum like a wand and flicked glittering silver fluid onto the soil. The mud foamed, writhed, swelled into a huge membranous bubble that burst, spilling forth a naked purple minotaur, six feet tall and fully formed.

"My priestly beast!" Swarovski declared. "As I am the god, and the dog, my body the one true temple, I declare you join your brothers and sisters in holy riot! Soon, we shall spread our message to the world!"

The inhuman crowd roared in joy and swept up the confused newborn. Swarovski set to wetting the dirt once again. Strass and Diamante watched creature after strange creature birthed from the earth and his secret formula.

"He's got a real front line assembly down there." Diamante frowned. "We should have brought more ammo."

"We need a diversion." Strass fingered her grenades.

111

At that moment, a raid siren blared, and three dozen Valkyrie figures rappelled down from a vast invisible dirigible lurking in the sky. They wore supple silver armor and purple berets and propelled themselves on wicked plasma skates that vaporized flesh and bone and burned the dirt to slag.

The Raspberry Berets zoomed round and round the amphitheatre, annihilating anyone they could throw beneath their glowing skates, a fist-pumping derby of death with Johnny Swarovski howling impotently in the eye of their storm. His acolytes were running and flapping and flopping from the amphitheatre, trampling each other, shrieking in unimaginable terror. In moments the Reverend Doctor would be the Berets' minionless prey.

"No way," Diamante vowed.

She drew her St. Vitus Dance and thumbed off the safety. The weapon hummed to life in her hand and spat jacketed lead at the invaders. A dozen heads exploded into red glitter before the others twigged to the threat above them.

The Berets scattered, reformed in smaller attack units, a military metastasis. Diamante picked them off with relentless precision. Strass stepped in when Diamante had to reload, hurling knuckleball grenades from each fist. Each bomblet went off with a sunburst flash and bone-pulping boom. The air filled with the stink of phosphorous and scorched hair.

The Berets' squad leader screamed down on them, one skate rising for a lethal roundhouse kick. Diamante cut her in half with a chainsaw barrage of bullets.

When the red mist cleared, Diamante and Strass were the only ones left standing amidst the amphitheatre carnage.

Just them ... and the Reverend Dr. Johnny Swarovski.

He turned toward them slowly, giving them a dazzling rockstar smile, letting his golden robe slowly fall open to reveal a perfect chest and promising package. "You girls are surely both my saviors. How can I ever repay you?"

Diamante pointed the Dance at his heart. "Get down on your knees and pray ...."

The Queen's secret service ambushed the girls the moment they tethered their lizard outside the palace.

"Hey now, hey now," Diamante complained as the guards frog-marched her and Strass into the throne room and forced them down on their knees. "What's this corrosion? We had a deal!"

"*Had.* Past tense." The Queen looked to the captain of her guard. "Have you the box? And the weapon?"

"Yes, Mum." He pushed his cape aside to reveal the St. Vitus Dance deactivated and holstered at his side, and then he gestured for his men to bring forth the medical stasis box. Johnny Swarovski stared at them balefully from behind the Plexiglas pane and mouthed silent obscenities.

"What about our promised payment?" Strass demanded. "We lost our bikes out there. We had *expenses.*"

"Leaving here with your lives should be payment enough," the Queen replied haughtily. "My advisors think I should simply have you both killed."

"That's a dirty deed!" Diamante fought against the men restraining her.

"Dirt cheap, too." Strass was very still.

"I am being most generous. Begone with you." The Queen waved her hand, and the guards hauled them back out to their giant lizard. A heavily armed squad escorted them to the city limits.

"Get out and don't come back!" the squad leader ordered. "You'll be shot on sight."

Diamante and Strass rode their lizard to the top of a nearby low mountain and stared out at the glittering spire of the castle. They could just barely make out the huge bulletproof picture window of the Queen's boudoir, where no doubt at that very minute Johnny's head was being put to salacious uses.

"What should we do?" asked Strass.

Diamante tipped her steely hat back and wiped her brow. "I reckon we go to Plan B."

Strass squinted at her. "You sure?"

"She's got it coming. And I expect Johnny'll prefer it this way."

Strass shrugged, dug in her jeans and pulled out a tiny black remote. Pressed the button. The boudoir window shattered outward as the microscopic, scanner-proof fusion device Strass had planted in Swarovski's neck stump exploded. Confetti of glass and steel sparkled in the midday sun as it rained down on the castle courtyard.

They watched the green smoke trailing up from the exploded window for a few moments before Strass spoke again: "Okay, so what now?"

"Wanna to go back to Cali?"

"Nah. Don't think so."

"How 'bout Kathmandu?"

Strass' face lit up. "You know? I've always wanted to!"

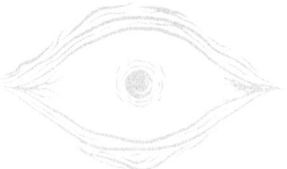

Tiger Girls vs. the Zombies

Eight months into the Apocalypse and we were all transformed: the living kept dying and the dead got no rest. The America of sitcoms and white-collar cubicles and Happy Meals had burned up like Los Angeles when the wildfires tore down from the hills. It burned up like my momma's brain after she caught the fever. It burned like the clove cigarettes we found in the pockets of the biker death cultists who tried to murder us in Reno.

Being good was the same as being dead. We were all gonna burn, either in this life or the next. But Tura? She knew how to live on fire.

Just a year ago, she was a researcher at UCLA, doing capital-ess Science by day and running triathlons on the weekends, casually busting down barriers just by living her life. I never had a chance to meet her there—I went to the university on a judo scholarship and meant to get a degree in nutrition. But I dropped out after two semesters when a guy at my gym recruited me for MMA. I couldn't turn down what seemed like an easy way to make some cash and get myself on TV. I can't kick worth a damn, but I'm good on the mat, and I won my share of prize money de-prettifying other girls' faces with your classic ground-and-pound. I always felt bad about that, afterward, and wondered what my life would have been like if I'd chosen brains over brawn. Heck, the zombie outbreak might have saved me; if I'd stayed in the game, sooner or later someone was gonna mess me up bad. And even if I didn't get my brain pulped in the ring, what would it look like at 40?

When I first laid eyes on Tura at the refugee camp, I thought she was a fighter like me. She had a warrior's walk and wary eyes. When I found out who she really was, I knew she'd been a great role-model. Way better than someone like me. Most any girl would see her and want to be her. Girls would want to be like her so bad that they'd stand up and blow off all the jerks who said girls couldn't do the math, couldn't crack the code, couldn't get strong, couldn't be people who mattered in the world.

I hoped some of those girls she'd inspired were still alive, and the jerks weren't. But like my daddy said: hope in one hand and spit in the other, and see which one gets wet first.

Now Tura was standing at the side of the road, staring out at the Rocky Mountains across the plain, dressed in oil-stained roughneck jeans and grimy boybeater and a pair of black leather chaps she'd taken off the skinniest dead guy in the Reno cult. Hands that used to carefully dissect brain tumors were now rough, calloused, her knuckles scarred like she'd been in more matches than I had. She kept our hair short with a gambler's straight razor. Months of hauling bodies and engines and fighting for our lives in the hard sun had given her a pair of guns she'd have never gotten on a Nautilus machine.

"You don't need him," I said.

She turned her hundred-mile stare on me. I could see her intellect like a vast, hot desert behind her stone-gray eyes. But not so much as a shadow of sanity seemed to soften her obsession.

She grinned at me, fresh bleeding cracks opening in her chapped lips. "I don't *need* him. That's a dead-cat fact, Johnnie. But I want that man so bad I can't think of anything else."

I squinted at her. "You figure he's really still alive?"

She pulled her satellite smartphone out of her pocket and brought up a text message: *OK 4 now. Nbdy hurt. Soldrs fled. Trapt at mtn lab. 2 mnths of food lft.*

"You sure that's Mickey?" I pressed.

She nodded. "I'm certain. He and his labmates are surrounded by zombies. He thinks maybe a hundred shamblers, a few dozen runners. He got his family in there before the soldiers who were supposed to protect them abandoned the place. They took all their weapons but a couple of .45s."

I sighed. We were supposed to be getting *away* from the damned undead, not heading straight for them. If I had any sense I'd have left right then, grabbed my bike and my half of the food we looted from the Safeway and kept on heading East.

The truth was, I needed Tura. She'd saved my butt more times than I could count. I'd only been able to repay the favor twice, and the idea of leaving our equation unbalanced like that just didn't sit right.

And, if you scratched past that skin, the bigger truth of it was that I loved her like she was family. More, maybe; I never got the feeling I was what my momma was hoping for when she birthed a girl. I never had a sister or a best friend growing up but I dreamed about that plenty. Never had much use for makeup or shopping or all that other girly stuff but it would have been nice to have someone to run around with. Someone to share my secrets with. Someone who made me feel like I belonged in the world.

When you spend your whole life out in the cold and finally find a nice warm fire, you want to stay near it, even if it stands a good chance of burning you.

"You in, Johnnie?" she drawled.

"You got a plan?" I replied.

She laughed that amazing cool laugh of hers. "Of course I have a plan, girl!"

Of *course* she did. And once she told me about it, I knew I'd be all in.

We zig-zagged across the landscape, gathering supplies and equipment, guided by the information she was able to pull down from the satellites that floated above all the dirtbound death and chaos like titanium angels.

Her plan started to go off the rails at a National Guard armory hidden up in the hills. The place was locked up tight, but once we broke in, we found the soldiers had stripped the place clean before they bugged out. Not so much as a shotgun to be found, much less the grenade launchers or M230 chain guns we'd been counting on scoring.

"Is there another place we can go for weapons?" I asked her.

She shook her head. "The talk on SurvivorNet is that all the other armories and bases in this half of the country have been looted. We'd have to steal weapons from a gang or militia, and I don't like our chances."

She thumbed through web pages on her phone, scowling. Then her frown changed to a look of intense calculation; it was an expression that simultaneously filled me with hope and worry.

"What is it?" I asked.

"There's something else we can try. It worked in Texas, and if those crazy rednecks pulled it off, I think we can, too."

Our first stop was a hardware store, where she loaded us up on rope, duct tape, sturdy canvas drop cloths and a couple of extra utility knives. Then we back-tracked to a Microcenter we'd passed in another town. The front windows had all been busted and the aisles were completely trashed. Unfazed, Tura grabbed her crowbar and headed straight to the back storeroom and started scanning the place with her flashlight.

"They usually keep the really good stuff locked up someplace secret." Her light lingered on what looked like nothing more than a custodian's closet. She stepped forward, tried the knob, discovered it was locked.

"Hmm." She knocked on the door, and I heard the solid rap of bone on steel. "I think we have a winner."

"What are you looking for?"

She stuck the crowbar's chisel tip in the door crack by the knob and started heaving. "You'll probably sleep better tonight if you don't know the details."

"I ... can't say I like that answer."

"Didn't expect you would. You just have to trust me for now."

The door gave with a squeal of metal and slammed open against the cinderblock wall. Tura shined her light inside. The first things I saw were racks and racks of custom-made gaming PCs, screaming fast monster computers with cases sculpted to look like alien beasts.

I cocked an eyebrow at her. "You planning to challenge the zombies to a Halo deathmatch?"

She laughed, stepped into the closet, and plucked a bright yellow software package off a lower shelf. I caught a glimpse of the words "HüDü Linux: Smartphone Edition" on the box before she shoved it into her rucksack. Tura grabbed some other boxes that looked like they contained some kind of wireless cards and stuck them in her bag as well.

"Let's roll," she said.

The next day, we pulled up in front of the Tranquility Creek Wildlife Center. The place was abandoned. Through the front gates, I could see dozens of empty animal cages, their galvanized steel doors swaying gently in the hot breeze.

"Lions and tigers and bears, oh my!" Tura clapped her hands like a little girl.

"Okay, seriously, what are you planning?" I asked.

She pulled one of the .22 rifles off the rack behind us and pressed it into my hands. "We're hunting big game. *But.* I don't want you to kill anything we find. We need to bring 'em back alive. Well. *Undead.* Shoot only if you have no choice; better to run first."

I followed her into the abandoned wildlife center and we began to sneak around, looking for … well, I still wasn't clear on that.

But when we came across a tiger pacing back and forth in a concrete drainage ravine, it was clear from Tura's reaction that we'd found it. The tiger was *huge*. She looked to be six feet long, not counting her tail, and close to 300 pounds. And her fur was in great shape. You wouldn't have known she was a zombie, except for her gray tongue and spoiled-milk eyes.

"Perfect." Tura gestured for me to follow her back to the truck, and we snuck away before the big cat had a chance to spot or smell us.

"Perfect for what?" I whispered back.

"Did you know that Siberian tigers prey on bears?" She had the serious tone of a nature show narrator.

"I did not know that, no."

"Truth. They eat the Russian version of grizzly bears. There isn't a land predator a tiger can't kill. And that especially includes humans."

Her plan was starting to take fuzzy shape in my head, but it still didn't make any sense to me. "So … you want to use that tiger to get rid of the zombies surrounding Mickey's lab?"

"Exactly," she replied. "And the tiger won't run out of ammo."

My face grew warm with frustration. "How in the name of sweet buttered corn are we going to keep that thing from killing *us* instead?"

Tura smiled in a way that a lot of folks might have found scary. "One thing at a time, doll."

Once we were back at the truck, Tura pulled out the yellow HüDü Linux box and the other stuff we'd gathered the past few days. She spent a good hour or so thumbing through the manual from the box and fiddling with her phone.

"Okay." She reached into the software box and pulled out a silvery metal rod, maybe six inches long and a half inch in diameter. "I think this is doable."

"What happens now?" I asked.

"Well, now you get to dust off your judo skills and shove this rod down the tiger's throat."

"… What? N-no way."

"Now, Johnnie. Don't be a fraidy-cat." Tura gave me a look that was one part *I dare you* and two parts *You owe me and you know it*.

Crap. I did owe her, and I did know it, but I wasn't suicidal. Or stupid. "What about that part where you said that tiger could kill a grizzly bear?"

"You just have to get it a couple of inches down her throat. Easy-peasy considering she'll be trying to eat you, right? Shouldn't take you but a few seconds."

"She'll tear me to pieces in just a few seconds!"

Tura sighed and pointed at the pile of canvas and the duct tape. "Johnnie. You'll be protected, don't worry."

Tura had me put on a set of the spare motorcycle leathers we'd salvaged—they were too big for me, but at least the pants stayed up—and then began to mummy me with wide strips of canvas and duct tape. By the time she was done, I was sweating buckets inside the leather and more than a little dizzy from the heat. But now I was wearing a pretty passable replica of a padded tactical training suit. I had a glimmer of hope it would survive ten seconds with a tiger.

"Are you gonna pass out?" she asked, peering at my face. It probably looked like a stewed tomato.

I shook my head.

"Can you bend your arms? Can you walk?"

I did an awkward macarena and waddled forward a few steps.

"Looking good!" She plopped a motorcycle helmet onto my head and cinched it under my swaddled chin. "Let's go."

As I waddled down into the ravine where the tiger paced, I felt like I was wading into the shark-infested water at Smyrna Beach wearing a chum bikini. But, as Tura had explained it, there wasn't any other way. We had to get the rod down the tiger's throat or we'd have no way to control it. And tranquilizers didn't work on zombies, and we didn't have any tranqs anyway. Nor were either of us good enough with a rope to do the cowgirl thing.

I stepped on a twig, and the tiger's head jerked around toward me, her black lips skinning away from algae-greened fangs the length of my fingers. Her pebble-rattling growl made me wish I'd taken a moment to go use the ladies' room, but it was too late for that now.

"Here kitty kitty kitty ...." I flipped my helmet's visor down.

The tiger—I was starting to think of her as Fluffy—sprang at me with speed I hadn't imagined. Three hundred pounds of fanged, clawed undead cat tackled me, and the air woofed out of my lungs as she slammed me down on the concrete. Fortunately I held onto the rod.

I'd been in this position before, back when super-heavyweight Amazonia Kartovsky took me down to the mat in our fight in Mexico. I wrapped my legs tight around the tiger's midsection so she couldn't rip my belly open with her back claws. And then before she could chomp down on my helmet I grabbed her snout with my left hand and pushed her away.

Fluffy roared at me and began to rip into the canvas on my shoulders with her front claws. The air filled with a flurry of canvas shreds. The blast of her breath seeped into my helmet and choked me. Cats don't have sweet exhalations at the best of times, but take the worst rotten-toothed, putrid-tuna, paint-peeling stink you've ever smelled and amp that to a level that threatens sanity and you'd have some idea of what that tiger's tonsil gas smelled like. In a word, *gross*.

I gritted my teeth against the bile rising fast in my throat and thrust the rod down Fluffy's slimy gullet, shoving my arm in all the way to my elbow. She buzz-sawed at my padding for another minute and then just stopped, her body going slack. I let go of the rod and squirmed out from under the big cat. I was sure I'd be sore tomorrow, but for now the adrenaline had me feeling no pain.

Tura whooped and ran down into the ravine to help me to my feet.

"That was stellar!" She slapped me on my back. "I just have to get the antenna software configured and run the OS installation and probably download some patches for her species and—uh oh."

She was looking down at me, wincing. I followed her gaze. The canvas on my right forearm was stained with blood around a puncture hole.

I'd been bitten.

I was all kinds of dead meat.

I started getting the chills as Tura helped me back to the truck. I knew from watching other people turn what would come next: terrible fever and thirst, convulsions, and then, finally, my eyes would go white and I'd pass into ravenous undeath.

"You should just kill me," I told her through chattering teeth.

She shook her head and began to cut the canvas, tape and sweat-soaked leather off me with a box knife. "I need your help. Let's see if you can ride this out tonight."

"Ride it out?" I stared at her. "Nobody ever rides this out!"

"It's a disease. Someone has to get better from it. Who's to say that won't be you?"

She got out our medical kit and started disinfecting my bite wound with alcohol and peroxide, as if those would make a difference.

"I'm toast," I whispered.

"Don't say that!" Tura glared at me as she slathered my wound with antibiotic cream and slapped on a bandage. "You find a way to live, Johnnie! Find a reason to live and hang on."

Looking into her fierce blue eyes, I didn't have to search very hard for my reason.

Tura pitched a tent, had me lie down inside in the shade and bound my hands and feet with nylon rope. I was too wrecked to argue.

"I'll check on you when I'm done with the tiger," she said. "Hang in there, okay?"

"Yes ma'am."

I closed my eyes and tried to find my inner calm. This was like any other fight. I had to get my immune system back in the game. Mind over matter, right?

But while I was meditating, sleep took hold of me, and my mind plunged down into the worst nightmares I've ever had. I was back in the ring, the canvas sticky with blood and scattered with bashed-out teeth and gobbets of flesh. There was a crowd watching me out there in the darkness beyond the spotlit ring, and from the growls and slobbering the spectators weren't people. I was naked, flat on my back, feeling more exposed than I had my entire life.

A zombie referee with a worm-eaten face stepped out from the shadowed corner and stood over me, bellowing a ten-count. I scrambled away from him, grabbed the ropes and hauled myself to my feet on shaky legs. The crowd roared, gutterally chanting the name of something no human could hope to pronounce.

"Fight!" the zombie referee shouted, pointing toward the center of the ring.

I turned and got my first good look at my opponent, and the sight of it made me feel as if my brain might melt. It was an utter abomination: a mutant head of tentacles and rasping hagfish mouths and bloody reptillian eyes all jumbled together in no natural pattern, a body sprouting horrible clawed arms. Only its legs looked vaguely human. And as I stared at it, it was getting bigger with every breath.

No way I wanted to go to the mat with that thing. How could I fight it? I needed a chainsaw or a flamethrower, and I didn't even have a pair of gloves.

"Fight!" roared the referee.

"Fight!" growled the crowd.

So I fought. I punched and I wrestled and I kicked and I bit. I went to the mat, I went to the ropes. Somehow, just as it was about to pin me or lay me out I managed to get free, and we'd start all over again. It just kept getting bigger and uglier and the crowd got louder, but I knew that if I quit I was dead, so I just kept swinging ....

I came out of the dream fighting the ropes binding my hands. There was something hard and cylindrical in my mouth, and my tongue was gummily stuck to it. Tura was kneeling beside me in the tent, looking down at me, clearly worried.

She reached down to pull the object out of my mouth, and I saw it was another metal rod like the one I'd shoved inside the tiger.

"You better not install Linux on me!" I yelled. "I'm strictly a Windows girl!"

Tura smiled like the light streaming in through the tent flap. "Thank God. You're okay."

"Okay" was kind of a relative thing. I'd been out of my mind with the fever for two days. I'd lost a bunch of weight and nearly died from dehydration; Tura had tried to get water into me but I kept spitting it out. Guess my brain thought it was fluid from the abomination I was fighting in the nightmare.

I sucked down five warm Gatorades as Tura filled me in on the rest. She told me she'd been tempted to put me out of my misery. But when my eyes stayed clear the first night, she stuck the extra rod in my mouth so that I wouldn't bite off my own tongue.

I did my best to get strong over the next three days, mostly resting and eating and doing some strength exercises and yoga when I could. At the end of it I could do a decent 50-yard sprint, climb a wall, and lift fifty pounds over my head. All without keeling over or barfing afterward. That's pretty much minimum fitness for the zombie apocalypse.

While I recovered, Tura spent time fine-tuning Fluffy's controls. She'd gotten the tiger working by the time I'd come out of the fever, but its movement was slow, robotic, jerky. By the time I was ready to hit the road, though, she had the tiger loping smoothly up and down the road, attacking tree trunks with great ferocity, and leaping back and forth over our truck.

It looked like we were as ready as we were going to be.

Three days later, we were on a bluff overlooking a big, square concrete building that sat in the middle of a barren plateau. Tura peered at it intently through a pair of binoculars. I could see hundreds of tiny figures milling around the building on all sides. Zombies.

"Yep. They're good and surrounded," she said.

"Why's his lab all the way out here?" I asked.

"It's a counter-terrorism facility. They come up with antidotes and vaccines for bioweapons. The bad guys cook it up, they break it down. They're handling some really hot stuff here, so they couldn't have the lab smack in a populated area. So, everybody's got a kind of rough commute."

Tura drove the truck down the butte onto the plateau. She took a moment to text Mickey, and then we got the tiger and our weapons out of the back. I had a 12-gauge loaded with buckshot and a .38 semiautomatic pistol. Tura had an AK-47 and twin .22 Colt revolvers. She set the tiger padding along by the truck and then we casually rolled toward the zombie horde.

Some of the undead turned their heads and began to shamble toward the truck when we were about 50 yards away. At 20 yards, Tura started punching keys on her smartphone and the tiger sprinted for the zombies.

Fluffy decapitated the first zombie with a single swipe and tore into the rest of the mob. Zombies fell dead all around her. It was like watching a hot knife go through a block of rancid butter.

"Faster, zombiecat! Kill! Kill!" Tura yelled.

But when Fluffy dove after what might have been the 200th zombie, an unusually tall and fat one, he fell across her back as he went down, and Fluffy's movements became erratic, jerky.

"Crap!" Tura exclaimed. "He dislodged her dorsal antenna. I gotta fix that—cover me!"

We jumped out of the truck and ran over to Fluffy. I plugged away at zombies with my pistol as Tura worked on getting the tiger back online.

I had to pause to reload, and in that moment a runner I hadn't seen grabbed me from behind and chomped my neck. I hollered, elbowed it off, and shot it right between the eyes. I touched my neck, and my hand came away wet with blood.

"I think I'm okay, guys. Honest." I was strapped to a dentist's chair in an observation room in the laboratory.

"I'm sure you'll be fine." Tura bandaged me up and gave me an antibiotic shot.

"We'll see," replied Mickey from the other side of the bulletproof glass. "Just try to relax."

"Okie-dokey." Mickey was a sweet hunk of scientist: he had a tight runner's body, long-lashed green eyes, an easy smile, and a mop of unruly black hair that practically said "Please run your fingers through me all the time, thanks!" He had the trifecta of brains, looks, and okay, maybe his personality wasn't exactly sparkling, but so far he didn't seem to be a jerk. Tura clearly didn't have eyes for anyone else.

I felt abandoned and miserable, and did the only thing I could do: I waited. And waited. And waited.

Six hours later, half the scientists still watching me were snoring in their folding chairs, so I cleared my throat and announced, "Guys. *Seriously.* I think I'm fine."

So they took my temperature, and drew a sample of my blood, and spent some time staring at it under a microscope.

"What do you think?" I asked.

"We think you're fine," Tura said.

"And I think we've finally got a source for good antibodies against this wretched plague," Mickey said, looking at me like I was a grand prize-winning lottery ticket. "Thanks to you, we're going to be able to save millions of lives."

"Sweet." I knew that saving humanity should have felt pretty darned satisfying, even if it *was* dumb luck. But in my loneliness, the miraculous victory just seemed hollow.

A young lab technician came into the room and began undoing my restraints. I hadn't really noticed her before, but she was red-haired, had a cute dusting of freckles, and was gazing at me with the kind of adoration that people usually reserved for movie stars. She was looking at me the way I'd probably been looking at Tura the past year.

"I think you're very brave," she whispered. "*Very* brave."

Me, a genuine hero? Apparently so. I smiled back at her. Suddenly the future seemed like a much brighter place.

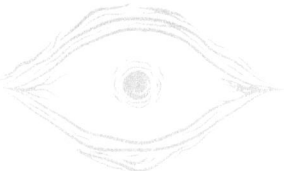

Repent, Jessie Shimmer!

My familiar Palimpsest kept insisting we go back to Madame Devereaux's house in the heart of bayou country to properly thank her for curing him of lycanthropy. And I kept telling him it wouldn't work; he was stuck in the form of a bear and would be awfully hard to explain to the townsfolk if we stopped to get a cake and flowers down at the Piggly Wiggly. Not to mention the difficulty of finding a rental car with a seat that could hold 800 pounds of grizzly.

Fate smiled on his determination a couple of weeks later. Well. Smiled is the wrong word. It was more a fately smirk. A newly-hired guard—one who apparently dozed off during his orientation on the strange creatures living in my father's castle—stumbled onto Pal after my familiar's morning swim in the moat. The guard, a kid barely out of school, freaked the heck out. And lit Pal up with his Taser. Which would have been an act of epic, life-ending stupidity on the guard's part had Pal been a normal grizzly bear. But instead of sending Pal on a man-slaying rampage, the powerful shock triggered his polymorphic enchantment and he began rapidly (and painfully) cycling through his past familiar bodies until the guard stopped zapping him.

When the smoke of burnt fur cleared, Pal was in his ferret form. Small. Cute. Non-threatening. Portable. Clearly it was time for a trip down south.

So just a few days later, I pulled my rented Dodge Ram truck up in front of Madame Devereaux's sprawling blue ranch house. The old witch was bent over the engine of her 1968 Volkswagen Beetle in the shade of the huge magnolia in her front yard. Her African mudcloth sundress and orange Crocs were smudged with black oil and red transmission fluid. Her granddaughter Shanique sat close by on a metal folding chair, holding a red toolbox at the ready, clearly trying to keep her brand new purple sneakers from getting greased.

"Hey there!" I waved to them as I got out of the truck with Pal perched on my shoulder.

Madame Devereaux straightened up, squinting at us from behind her thick, old-fashioned bifocals. "Jessie Shimmer, is that you?"

"Yes ma'am."

"Ain't you got that paw of yours fixed yet?" She pointed at the gray satin opera glove covering my left hand and forearm.

"Oh, it's fixed. No more hellfire." I pulled down the cuff of the burn-proof glove to show her my pale, luminous flesh. I was glad it was closer to normal. Having a hand made out of flame is great if you're trying to barbecue things, but it's lousy for pretty much anything else. It's especially hard to hold onto anything when your hand doesn't have any bones; I'd had to rely on my natural talent for spiritual extension, a type of parakinesis, and even that failed if I wasn't paying attention. My Frisbee game sucked hard.

"It still looks weird, so I still keep it covered up," I finished.

"What you doing here? Your daddy need something?"

"No ma'am ... Pal here wanted to come back to see if there was anything we could do to thank you for curing him."

The old lady seemed simultaneously flustered and annoyed. "I done told you I don't need no payment for that!"

"It's not about payment, ma'am ... he just wants to do something to thank you."

We went back and forth for a couple of minutes in gentle argument until Shanique finally said, "What about your healing stone, Grandma?"

"Hm." Madame Devereaux rubbed her chin. "I reckon gettin' that back would be a fine thing."

"Healing stone?" I asked. "Where is it?"

"Boudreaux Metier borrowed my best crystal to cure some of his coon hounds what came down with distemper last year. It's a relic your daddy gave me, a dark purple amethyst carved in the shape of the goddess Hygieia. 'Bout four inches high. Boudreaux said he'd just be a couple days with it but he ain't brung it back yet. I tried to call him on his cell, but I reckon he dropped it down the sump again. He lives a ways back in the bayou and I just ain't been up for going out there on my own."

She paused, wincing. "Boudreaux always wants you to set a spell, see, and try whatever vile rotgut he's brewed up from his still. I think that boy's done burned out his tastebuds. Anyway. If y'all were to go get that stone back for me, I'd surely appreciate it."

"Consider it done," I replied.

It was almost evening before Madame Devereaux's directions got me on the road to Boudreaux's place out in the bayou. She'd warned me that my truck's GPS wouldn't be much good, and sure enough, the device was telling me I'd reached a dead end even though I could see a straight path of mud-reddened gravel parting the thick forest of pine trees and cypresses. I could have cast a spell to track him, but that required a bit of Boudreaux's hair or a toenail clipping or a personal item, and Madame Devereaux didn't have so much as a mason jar of his moonshine.

We followed the road down into a darkening hollow, then up onto a small hill where we encountered the real dead end. A couple hundred yards away, I could see an Army green house lurking in a clearing. The two-story plantation style home had seen better days; the double wraparound porches were warped and Spanish moss dripped from the upper railings. A couple of rusty cars on blocks and cords of firewood were piled in the yard around the building.

"I can't say I like the look of the place," Pal told me telepathically, craning his neck out the window and sniffing the piney air. "I smell carrion."

"Boudreaux's got coon hounds," I replied. "He's a hunter. Of *course* you smell dead things. He's probably got a critter pit or something to dispose of carcasses."

Despite my words, far more sinister possibilities were already crowding in my mind. So after I killed the engine I went to the trunk to get out my Mossberg shotgun and a sheathed knife I could slip inside my boot. A girl can't be too careful. My defensive magic is pretty decent, but sometimes there's just no substitute for a firearm or a blade.

I slung the Mossberg over my left shoulder and Pal perched on my right, his whiskers twitching with anxiety. Still, he didn't complain. I began to make my way through the litter of leaves, small branches, and scattered car parts toward the house. Halfway there I stepped over the crumbling remains of a low stone wall that, once I'd crossed it, we both realized contained some kind of warding magic.

"Oh dear," said Pal.

I reached down, picked up a couple of tinder-dry pine needles, and spoke a couple of old word for "flame". The charm seemed to stick in my throat. Nothing happened. Not so much as a spark or wisp of smoke. Crap. I'd run into a magic-dampening field before; it had been powered by captive witches and wizards trapped in a thrall circle. Not an easy piece of spell work. The stones behind my feet didn't feel strong enough to be the source.

Pal was staring at the unlit needles in my hand. "This does *not* bode well."

"No, it doesn't," I thought back to him. "But Boudreaux's a friend of Madame D. ... if he's in trouble she'd want to know. Especially if the trouble could spill over to her and Shanique."

Still, it was time to do a couple of quick tests before we went any further. My left eye was an enchanted stone; I blinked through a couple of views to confirm that the suppression field wasn't affecting items imbued with permanent magic.

"My ocularis is good, so whoever's casting this isn't that powerful." I reached into my pocket, found a lighter, flicked it with my thumb. A sturdy little flame flashed to life. "And we've got fire. So my shotgun will still work. It'll be fine."

We continued on to the house. I kept the shotgun slung at what I hoped looked like a casual angle, but I could bring it up in a hurry if I needed to. If we were being watched, I didn't want to seem threatening. We got to the front of the house, and went up the creaky, mossy steps onto the worn porch. I knocked on the brown steel front door. Waited. No answer.

"Hello, Mr. Metier, are you there?" I called. "Anybody home?"

I was about to knock again when I heard the deadbolt slide back and the door swung open to reveal a tall man dressed in a tattered black dress shirt and muddy black tactical pants. His hair was a filthy, gray-streaked blond mane and his long beard was turning into dreadlocks. He didn't look or smell like he'd showered in months. And it was more than just dirt, old sweat, and crusty underwear; he wore an unmistakable stench of meaty rot.

"Whatchu want, girl?" He had the voice of a man who'd smoked a million cigarettes, and glared down at me with eyes the color of an algae-sheened cesspool.

"Madame Devereaux sent me." I couldn't keep my voice steady. "Are you Boudreaux Metier?"

He shook his head, and as his beard moved I saw that his black shirt was topped with a stained clerical collar. "I'm Brother Hiram. Boudreaux is busy with the Lord's work."

"Jessie." Pal's voice was tight with fear. "This fellow doesn't have a heartbeat. We should go. *Now*."

"The Lord's work?" The magic suppression spell, no doubt. If this guy had enslaved Boudreaux, he probably wasn't working alone. I had the horrible feeling I didn't have nearly enough ammo. Time to call for help. I fixed a smile on my face and carefully backed away. If I got past the first car on blocks I could sprint for the stone fence and be past the wards in maybe five seconds. "He must be real busy. I'll just come back later, okay?"

Brother Hiram opened the door wide and strode toward me, his frown deepening. "You say Madame Devereaux sent you?"

"Yes." I half-stumbled off the porch and down the stairs. Maybe I should drop the neighborly pretense and just shoot him. But that might not stop him. I didn't know what he was. He seemed too smart and self-aware to be a zombie. A headshot would just annoy a vampire. I couldn't remember what to do with a ghoul or a revenant. Heart? Stomach? Decapitation?

"That Madame Devereaux is a hoodoo witch, ain't she? That must mean you're some kinda witch, too." Brother Hiram was staring at my gloved hand as if it still glowed with hellfire.

I raised the shotgun to my shoulder, aiming at his throat. If I got him with a good solid blast under the jaw, maybe I could pop his skull off. "Don't come any closer."

"I reckon the Bible's pretty clear on the subject of witches." He stopped coming toward me, but didn't raise his hands or avert his stare. "The good Lord said in Exodus 22:18, 'Thou shalt not suffer a witch to live.'"

Then there came a rustling all around, the sound of cold bodies unfolding themselves from leaf-covered shallow graves and straightening up on dead legs. I turned to see how many creeps were coming toward me; a quick glance around showed at least thirty undead men in ragged clothes shambling toward me. Crap.

I only looked away from Brother Hiram for maybe a second, but that was enough. He rushed forward and grabbed the barrel of my shotgun with a strength I didn't imagine he possessed. Before he jerked it out of my hands I managed to pull the trigger, hoping to get him in the face, but the blast went wide. My ears rang.

Hiram held the Mossberg high, swung it around and slammed the butt into my sternum. Right over my heart. The blow woofed the air out of my lungs and hurt like hell. I stumbled backward, bright stars sparking in my vision, but managed to stay on my feet. Pal's little claws dug into my shoulder as he scrambled for purchase.

"I ain't in a mood to suffer the likes of you." Hiram glowered at me, gripping my shotgun in his dirt-streaked fists.

His ragged mob was nearly on me. I had time to do exactly one thing, so I grabbed Pal with both hands and tossed him up into what I hoped would be safety in the branches of the nearest cypress.

"Go get help!" I thought to him as I turned to face the men surrounding me.

"What am I, Lassie?" His voice teetered on the edge of hysteria. "We're out in the middle of nowhere—how am I supposed to get any help?"

I kicked a man dressed in a rotting flannel shirt and camouflage pants; his lips had been mostly eaten away from his face by maggots. "Call Madame Devereaux! She's in my contact list ... if she doesn't answer, try my brother!"

"And your cell phone is where?"

"Glove box!" I punched a guy who had pus-filled holes where his eyes should have been.

"Is the truck locked?"

It was. I swore, kicking away a guy who had a spiked billy club strapped to the decaying stump of his right arm.

"Jeepers creepers, Pal, go find a car battery and lick it or something! Embiggen yourself and break in!" I thought back.

"Y'all stop foolin' around and git 'er down, already!" Brother Hiram barked.

The zombies dogpiled me, pressing me down into the leaves and slimy mud. I thought I would pass out from their weight and stench. A moment later, one of them had looped a rope around my neck and they were dragging me through the yard as I gagged and fought for breath.

They pulled me up onto my knees beside a huge woodpile and held me there, my arms outstretched. I didn't fight them, taking a moment to try to get my bearings and breath back. I was completely surrounded. I'd have a chance if I could just get my shotgun back, but without it, I was pretty much screwed. The hidden boot knife's sheath was jammed painfully into my calf. No way to reach it.

I heard the sound of heavy footsteps in the leaves, and the mob parted to let Brother Hiram through. He stood in front of me, still holding my shotgun. His face was grim. "You are a witch and an abomination unto the eyes of the Lord. But ye shall repent, and before this day is over you will be calling the Lord's name with all your heart and He will welcome you with open arms into His kingdom. Eternal salvation will be my gift to you."

I dearly wanted to tell him in graphic anatomical detail exactly where he could stick his salvation. But I had a rare moment of prudence and realized that anything I had to say would just make things worse. So I held my tongue, watching to see what their next move would be.

Hiram nodded at his rotting crew. "Git 'er ready."

Two of them carried over a 6"x6" square wooden post beam. A pair of iron D rings had been securely screwed into the middle of the rough-hewn beam, as if it was supposed to be hung someplace. Someone had routed a series of well-worn grooves a few inches from each end. The wood was mildewed; it looked like it had been spending a lot of time near the water, and it was stained with something dark and rusty. Old blood. The beam was a bit longer than the width of my outstretched arms; I guessed it was probably six feet even. Six by six by six. What the hell were they going to do?

Dead hands pulled me up, turned me over, and threw me down on the beam, binding me tightly by my wrists to the wood with coarse sisal rope that fit neatly into the grooves. My stomach churned as I realized what they had planned.

"We used nails for the first couple of crucifixions," Brother Hiram said. His expression had changed now that I was seemingly helpless; he was looking down at me with something that almost seemed like kindness in his dead eyes. "But nails make the wood too weak after a while, and I seen a couple of people pull off the nails, and then the whole thing's over too quick. Rope's better all the way around."

Hiram paused. "I reckon God wants us all to suffer so we'll appreciate Heaven when it comes along. So I ain't doing my bit for the good Lord if you die too fast. You need time to really reflect on the pain you'll be feeling and accept him into your heart, and I aim to give that to you."

They hauled me up to my feet and kicked me forward onto a muddy path that wound down through the trees. The guy in front of me was shirtless, and a huge swath of flesh was missing from his side. I could see nearly all his ribs. In my light-headed terror his bones reminded me of a xylophone or marimba, and suddenly the Violent Femmes' "Gone Daddy Gone" was playing inside my head.

The wooden crosspiece was a hell of a thing to carry. It weighed probably fifty or sixty pounds, which normally wouldn't have been much of a problem if I just had decent grip on it, or even if they'd put it up on my shoulders. But the damn thing was dragging halfway down my back, twisting all my arm joints out of their sockets. They'd bound the scratchy ropes so tightly that my flesh hand was turning puffy and purple; I didn't know what my eerie hand looked like beneath the glove. I couldn't pull the crosspiece up, I couldn't put it down; I was constantly off balance. When I fell, they'd haul me up and shove me down the path again.

By the time we got to the edge of the swamp, I was half-blind from exhaustion and perspiration, gasping for air like I'd just run a marathon. My jeans and tee shirt were covered in red mud and dead leaves and pine needles. My arms and shoulders ached horribly, and my hands had gone completely numb.

"Git 'er on out there," Brother Hiram said.

The dead men pushed me out into the chest-deep water, and my vision cleared enough to see the tall wooden post set out in the middle of the swamp; it looked like a stolen telephone pole that they'd stripped of its original hardware. A pair of newer steel hooks was bolted to it about three feet from the top. On each side of the tall post were short steps made of cypress logs.

They pushed me out to the post, and the tallest of the men grabbed each end of the crosspiece and hauled it and me up out of the water. After a couple of shoulder-wracking tries they got the crosspiece hung from the hook. They splashed back to shore, leaving me hanging out there in the damp heat and eerie quiet.

My booted feet dangled about two feet from the deep green water; I tried to grip the pole with my legs to take the weight off my arms, but the wood was too slippery. It smelled like they'd smeared it with axle grease. The sun beat down on me, merciless as Brother Hiram, and mosquitoes whined in my ears. My arms were screaming, and I could already feel the hang-strained muscles in my chest beginning to spasm.

I closed my eyes, concentrating.

Pal, are you there? I thought. *I could use some help over here. Pal?*

No response. Either he was too far away for telepathy, or ... I didn't want to think about the alternatives.

I'm so screwed, I thought.

A low roar rolled across the water. It sounded like a huge crypt slab being dragged across the hollow marble floor of a mausoleum. I was suddenly aware that, beneath the stench of the dead men, I could smell the sharp rankness of reptile offal.

My skin broke out in goosebumps despite the heat. I scanned the water, spotted what I first thought was the fat trunk of a downed tree. And then realized it was moving. Toward *me*.

The swimming gator was nearly as big as a dragon. It was easily twenty feet long and had a maw of sharp, jagged teeth the size of steak knives. And, as it came closer, I saw that it had milky white eyes, and patches of its thick hide were missing from its back, revealing grey leathery muscle beneath.

Somebody started spewing profanity and shrieking about zombie gators. It took me a couple of seconds to realize I was the one making all the noise.

"Taking the Lord's name in vain won't help you none," Brother Hiram called. "You best start repentin'. I gave ol' Rufus there a sacrament of my own blood, and he's an instrument of God now."

I squeezed my eyes shut and took a deep, painful breath. *Stop panicking. Panic won't help.*

What could I do? For the first time, I wished my left hand were still a torch of cursed hellfire; at least then I'd have a shot at burning the ropes and freeing myself. The knife in my boot was plenty sharp enough, but even if I had the circus freak flexibility to swing my foot up to my hand, my fingers were too numb to grip anything.

What about the anti-magic field? Those took a fair bit of juice to maintain, and I didn't see any ward stones along the banks. I tried speaking a couple of simple charms for lights in the air, but I got that same sticking-in-my-throat sensation and the words failed. Crap.

I was running out of options. My stone eye worked, but it was only good for different sight; I couldn't shoot laser beams with it or anything. I made a mental note to ask my father about getting an upgrade.

"Rufus ain't had no food for a while so he can't jump real high," Brother Hiram said. "Probably he'll only take your feet at first. It'll take him a while to chew those fancy boots of yours, I 'spect, but once he's got your meat in him he'll get friskier. He'll get your knees on his next jump, and after that it's a mite hard to predict. I seen him get hold of one feller's innards on the third jump and start windin' 'em out of his body like he was unspooling a hose. You shoulda heard that feller start prayin'! It warmed my heart to see him find God like that."

I swore in frustration and slammed my head back against the wood.

"But don't you worry none," Brother Hiram added. "If he takes a mite too much of your giblets I can give you a sacrament so you'll stay awake. Even at his friskiest Rufus is a little too big to get more'n chest high. As long as your head's still on your shoulders, you'll be able to keep repentin' all night."

Christ on a crutch. Well, at least he'd confirmed how I could kill these creeps. If I ever figured out a way off this damn pole. I wondered briefly if Brother Hiram meant to come out to where I was hanging to give his "sacrament", but then I saw one of the zombies hand him a case that contained a black Spyder air rifle, a tub of bright orange paintballs, and an embalming syringe. Hiram took out the syringe and plunged the thick needle into his own neck. Once he'd filled the barrel with his tarry blood, he began injecting it into the paintballs.

Well. That would do it. He'd just have to get some of his blood in my mouth or on an open wound to turn me. An easy shot from where he was, supposing his eyes were 20/20. I was screwed a hundred ways to Sunday.

The monstrous gator was still cruising toward me; it was maybe fifty feet away now. The rotten-fish stench of him was starting to make my eyes water. I wracked my brain, trying to figure out what I could do. If I could just get to the knife in my boot, I could get myself untied and climb the top of the pole—it didn't look like they'd greased the wood above my head—but that would take magic.

I stared resentfully at my left hand, wishing I could get the damn thing to flame up one last time. Before it had been cursed fire it had been gone completely, courtesy of having been bitten off by a demon. At least when I was nothing more than an amputee I could still grip things, courtesy of my parakinesis, and nobody could tie my missing arm up—

Wait a minute, I thought, my heart beating faster. *Who's to say that couldn't work now?*

Parakinesis was a kind of magic, sure, but it was a natural talent I'd improved with practice. It wasn't a spell. If my eye still worked, my parakinesis should, too. The trouble was, I'd never tried to disconnect my spiritual extension from my flesh.

Rufus was less than twenty feet away. I didn't have a choice—I *had* to make this work.

Okay. I closed my eyes and took a deep breath. I concentrated on my left arm, the feel of the ropes biting into my gloved wrist, the hard wood against my elbow, the sun burning my bared skin. I lifted my knees, imagining that I was kneeling on solid ground, imagining that the ropes just weren't there. I pictured myself dropping my freed left arm down to my boot. And then I could feel my fingers sliding down into the leather shaft, grasping the handle of the knife, and pulling it out.

The huge gator let loose a tooth-rattling roar right below me, and I don't think I've been so startle-scared in my whole life. It literally spooked me out of my skin. I scrambled up to the top of the pole, clinging for dear life with the knife clenched in my fist, and it took me a long second to realize that my consciousness had entirely left my flesh. My real body hung there limply, unconscious, not breathing. I saw myself in spiritual form as a faint, translucent glow. A glance at the dead men on the shore told me they couldn't see me like this.

White-eyed Rufus heaved himself out of the water and made a snap for my swaying feet, missing by a couple of inches. Crap. I had to hurry if I didn't want to become a permanent ghost haunting this swamp. But while I was a ghost, I was freed from not just flesh but most physics. I knelt on the crosspiece and began to saw at the ropes binding my flesh wrist to the wood. The last strand abruptly snapped, and my body swung down, perilously close to Rufus' jaws. Almost as bad, the torsion on my still-bound arm was bending my elbow the wrong way and I worried it was about to snap. I grabbed myself by the back of my tee shirt, and hauled my body up onto the crosspiece with one hand while I slashed the remaining ropes with my left.

A sudden dizziness washed over me; I realized my unconscious body's face was turning blue. I pitched forward, back into my flesh, and awoke coughing and gagging, strained lungs burning, desperately grabbing at the pole to keep myself from tumbling off the wobbly crosspiece to the waiting teeth below. My arms were trembling, my hands barely able to grip the wood. The knife, meanwhile, had splooshed down into the swamp.

A bloody paintball whizzed past my right ear.

"I gotta say, I seen a whole bunch o' witches, but I ain't never seen 'em pull a trick like that. I guess I need to have a talk with ol' Boudreaux about the importance of the Lord's work. You might be feelin' right clever right now, but I got a flame-thrower back at the house. We'll see how you pray when I set your pretty little face on fire."

I felt exhausted and light-headed; I didn't think I could spiritually project myself again for a while. I scooted around so the bulk of the post was between me and Brother Hiram. Hopefully it would block most of his shots. I didn't think he could really hurt me unless he got blood in my mouth or eyes, but it was better not to take the risk. For all I knew, he had laced his paintballs with shards of glass or something else to cut skin.

I closed my eyes again and concentrated on reaching out to my familiar. *Pal, are you out there? Pal?*

Jessie, I couldn't get through to anyone on your phone. His voice was distorted in my mind. I hoped that meant he'd been able to change his form. *But I have another idea. Where are you?*

Down at the swamp, I replied. *Hurry!*

Rufus bellowed again and began to slam the post with the side of his enormous head, trying to shake me off my perch. Brother Hiram fired a couple more paintballs at me that went wide. Undead sometimes don't have very good daytime vision, and that was a small mercy.

Suddenly, I heard an even louder, bearish roar from the trees above us. My heart jumped with surprise and hope. Pal must have found a battery with a really good charge and had managed to get himself into his form that blended all his past bodies: he was a gigantic shaggy spider with a four-eyed head that looked like a saber-toothed tiger's by way of a mescaline hallucination. In his forelegs, he gripped a pair of rusty machetes.

"Yeah, Pal!" I hollered. "Kick their asses!"

Pal galloped down on Brother Hiram's crew, swinging the blades right and left. I saw arms and heads fly along with sprays of black blood. But then the ghoulish preacher grabbed my shotgun and started blasting away at my familiar. Pal shrieked as buckshot bit into in his side, but he grabbed one of the zombies and threw him on top of Hiram, knocking him down. The weapon flew out of the preacher's hands and landed in a thatch of swamp azalea partly overgrown with kudzu vines.

I swore. Adrenaline flooded my bloodstream, giving me energy I thought I'd lost for the day. I had to help Pal: I had to get to shore, somehow.

Rufus was leaping at me again, his claws scrabbling at the pole as if he hoped to be able to climb the wood. His mouth was open wide, gaping like a baby bird's.

I climbed higher on the pole, held on for dear life, gritted my teeth, and used my legs to lift the wooden crosspiece off the hooks. And at that moment, Brother Hiram finally got his wish: I started praying.

"Please, God, let this work," I said to the sky, my whole body shaking with fear and exertion. "Please, please, please."

Then I dropped one knee, letting the wooden bar tumble down. Bullseye! Rufus gave a strangled roar as the wood rammed right down his gullet, and he fell backward, furiously shaking his head to try to dislodge the crosspiece.

It wouldn't distract him long. I jumped down into the water and swam as hard as I could toward Pal, who was hacking up another zombie. Brother Hiram had almost pulled my shotgun free of the kudzu.

Cursing, I surged out of the water and kicked Hiram in the small of his back. He stumbled but didn't fall, and swung the shotgun toward me. I was ready for him this time; I grabbed the barrel and slammed my knee into his groin. There was the sound of old bone cracking, and his grip loosened enough for me to wrestle the weapon away from him.

And then I did what I meant to do in the first place: I jammed the shotgun under his chin, closed my mouth, and pulled the trigger. His head came apart like a rotten watermelon and his body collapsed like a sack of garbage straight down to the mud.

The zombies fighting Pal abruptly dropped their fists and weapons, seeming confused and unfocused. Most of their cunning and motivation had apparently come from Brother Hiram. I looked out at the swamp; Rufus had stopped struggling against the wood stuck in his throat and once again resembled nothing more than a half-submerged log.

"Are you okay?" I called to Pal.

"For now." Pal lopped off a couple more heads, then tossed me his second blade. "I'm sure my blood's been tainted, but I should be able to keep my mind about me for a few more hours. And I know Madame Devereaux can cure what my own powers cannot. Let's finish these fellows off before they get hungry and decide to wander into town."

I helped Pal decapitate the rest of the gang, and then we went back up to the trail to the old house.

Brother Hiram had left a couple of sentries behind, but they were just as dumb and befuddled as the others now that he was dead. Once we'd put them out of their misery, Pal stuck his tongue in a handy electrical outlet and shocked himself back down to his ferret form. We searched the house, and found both Boudreaux Metier and Miz Deveraux's healing crystal up in the attic.

Boudreax wasn't undead, exactly, but he was agonizingly thin and sick-looking. Hiram had chained him to the floor and drugged him into a trance with whatever the old-fashioned glass IV was dripping into his arm. He was reciting the same spell over and over through his chapped, blistered lips: this was the source of the anti-magic field.

The carved healing crystal sat discarded on a nearby set of dresser drawers, surrounded by ceramic knickknacks and sundry other junk. The image of Hygeia looked enough like the Virgin Mary at first glance that Brother Hiram probably never realized what it was. I grabbed the crystal and spoke the magic word Madame Devereaux had given me to activate it. It glowed blue in my hand.

I knelt beside Boudreaux, gently pulled the needle from his arm, and pressed the statuette against the suppurating ulcer it had made. It glowed brighter, and his deathly pallor flushed to an almost-healthy pink. He stopped chanting, his jaw falling slack. A snore rattled in his throat.

"Hey Boudreaux." I patted his cheek. "Wake up."

His eyes popped open. After a moment of unfocused, chain-fighting panic, he seemed to see me, realize I wasn't a zombie, and relaxed.

"Where's Hiram?" he croaked.

"Dead," I replied.

"Good." He coughed. "That's the *last* time I invite my damn in-laws over for Thanksgiving! You wouldn't have a Dr. Pepper, would ya?"

"I saw some in the kitchen." I began to undo his chains. "Let's get you downstairs, and then we'll all go over to Madame Devereaux's."

Boudreaux stared at the crystal in my hand. "Aw, crap, I was s'posed to get that back to her!"

"Don't worry about it; I'm pretty sure she'll understand that you've been a little tied up over here ...."

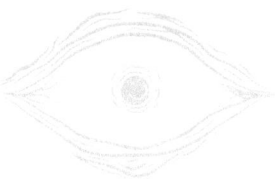

The Leviathan of Trincomalee

Thilini Rothschild saw the green fireball streaking across the sky above the coconut palms before her father did. "Look, Papa!"

"Why, that's an extraordinary meteor! I've never seen one of such color." He peered out at the night sky through his workshop window. "It's fortunate that will crash far out in the Indian Ocean and not in a city!"

She gazed at the fireball's sparkling emerald tail, entranced and yet feeling a bit crestfallen. "I hoped it was falling star so I could wish upon it."

"Why, I'm sure a fine meteor such as that is just as wish-worthy!"

So she closed her eyes and thought, *I wish for an adventure!*

Three years later, Thilini had forgotten all about the meteor. She woke before the first crows of her mother's junglefowl, wound on her favorite green sari, and slipped out to the kitchen to gather some cold chickpea fritters and jackfruit in a basket. Her father would still be at his workshop by the harbor; no doubt he'd been working on his wireless telegraph machine all night. He'd probably forgotten to eat.

Excitement jittered in her stomach. Today was the day the *Southwind* would return, her hold creaking with goods. If the special gears and glass panels her father had commissioned from his partners in Switzerland arrived with it, that meant they might finally be able to assemble the submarine prototype she and her father had been working on for the past year. Thilini couldn't wait to see the ocean from beneath the waves.

She hefted the reed basket over one shoulder, slipped into the sandals her mother made her leave by the front door, and ran down the wagon-rutted road to the harbor shops. To her surprise, a stout, balding man was standing in the

141

shop, arms crossed. Her father frowned up at him from his workbench, his eyes shadowed in the flickering candlelight. Biting her lip, she pushed open the front door, quietly so the bells wouldn't jingle.

"You're wasting your talents here," the stranger lectured in German. "You need to go back to Europe. Or at least come to our estate in Kandy."

Her father pulled off his wire-framed round glasses and pinched the bridge of his nose. His long curly brown hair had come loose from his queue. He looked exhausted. "I'm fine, Martin. The clean air here suits me more than the noise and stink of Frankfurt or London."

He looked past Martin and his eyes focused on Thilini.

"Ah, you brought breakfast?" he asked her in Tamil.

"Yes, Papa. Who is this?"

"Your uncle Martin," he continued, still speaking in her native language. "Pay him and his unpleasantness no mind."

"Yes, Papa."

"'Attān'?" Martin said, repeating her endearment, staring at Thilini. Recognition seemed to dawn; he grimaced in disgust. He stared back down at her father, eyebrows raised. "Are you this little pickaninny's sire?"

Her father turned red as a berry, his fists clenching in his lap. "I'll not have you speak about my daughter in such a debased fashion."

"Debased?" Martin exclaimed. "It is you who have debased our family! Rothschilds dance in the courts of every ruler in Europe, and yet here you are, tinkering in the sand, breeding like a mongrel with the first brown bitch who wiggles her tail at you."

It was Thilini's turn to feel the blood rise in her face. She could bear insults to herself with all the quiet grace her parents had taught her, but she would not stand by while this stranger spoke so badly of her mother. But her father responded before she could open her mouth.

"I have lived upon five continents." Her father's voice shook with rage. "And Thilini's mother is the finest woman I have ever met. None of the simpering court ladies you and your brothers deemed so suitable as matches have half the beauty, intelligence, or courage of my dear Anula."

"Indeed," Thilini replied in her best German. "If my mother is such a poor match for my father, I should be a useless idiot, should I not? So, test me. Ask me any question you like, in any language you like."

Martin was clearly surprised she knew German at all. "Who's the tsar of Russia?"

"Alexander the Third."

"And the President of the United States?"

"Grover Cleveland. Please, do ask me something difficult, dear Uncle."

Martin frowned. "What's the square root of eighty-one?" he asked in French.

"Nine," she replied in English.

"What are the components of black powder?" he asked in German.

"Sulfur, charcoal, and saltpeter," she replied in French. "I can make you some if you like. The recipe is easier than my mother's fish soup."

"Why doesn't your father's wireless telegraphy machine work?"

She smiled at him. "And now you're fishing for trade secrets, Uncle."

Her uncle stared at her. "How old are you?"

"I shall be thirteen in two months."

After Martin left, her father fussed at her a bit for speaking so boldly to her uncle, but clearly he was proud of her. They ate the breakfast she brought, and then he sent her down to the docks with their portable telegraph prototype. It was based on some of the correspondences he'd had with the American inventor Brooks. The device almost worked, but the power supplies they'd tried were insufficient for the components.

"I'm sure the new electrochemical cells will do the trick. It's just a matter of fine-tuning the equipment," he said as he loaded the sixty-pound rig onto her little palmwood wagon.

"Can we make it smaller?" she asked doubtfully.

He laughed. "Reliability first. Miniaturization second."

Thilini hauled the wagon down to the docks and took up a vantage point where she could keep watch for the tall sails of the *Southwind*. Occasionally, part of a telegraph would come through; she'd transcribe the message and jot down the time in her notebook. The first time they'd gotten anything at all to transmit and be received through thin air, they'd both been overjoyed. But getting an entire message to go through over distances more than ten feet or so had proved a confoundingly difficult challenge.

Science, she mused, involved an awful lot of waiting and doing-over.

Her reverie was broken by the shouts of men. She stood. The *Southwind* had sailed into view … but she was too low in the sea, and listing so far to one side she looked in danger of capsizing. Had the ship broken its hull on a coral reef?

"She's taking on water fast!" the stevedore shouted. "Every man with a boat, get out there! We need to get that cargo off!"

Two hours later, Thilini stood with her father as two deeply tanned dockworkers pulled the precious Swiss crates from the deck of a patamar that had been pressed into rescue duty. The crates were so waterlogged that she would not have been surprised to hear fish flopping inside them. The glass would be fine, provided it had not been mishandled, but she cringed at the corrosion the seawater would wreak on the delicate gears if they were not carefully rinsed, dried, and re-oiled.

"Please, get these back to my shop as quickly as you can," he told the men of the hired wagon.

"Yes, Herr Rothschild." They quickly set to loading up the crates.

The stevedore approached them, shaking his head. He was a small, wiry man who looked Tamil but he wore a Catholic rosary over his loose cotton shirt and had a slight Portuguese accent. "A third of the cargo lost, and five sailors sent to the Almighty. The ship can't be repaired in the water, so we need to find some way to haul 'er in to dry-dock before she sinks. And I ain't convinced she won't just sink."

"Was it a reef?" Thilini asked.

"If only!" the stevedore replied. "We could dodge a reef, but this … well, come see. Perhaps your papa can make heads or tails of this deviltry."

Further down, another boat had come in bearing a broken plank from the hull. Not broken, she realized. Something had bitten it in half! Imbedded in the stout English timber was a shark's tooth of far greater size than any she'd imagined. The biggest one she'd seen until then was about the size of a gold sovereign coin.

"Mein gott," her father breathed. He laid his hand beside the protruding tooth; it was larger than his palm and outstretched fingers. "What leviathan could grow such a fang? Some type of cachalot whale?"

"*Carcharodon carcharias*," came a voice behind them.

Thilini turned. Trincomalee's resident naturalist, the retired physician Edward Kelart, was gazing at the tooth with grave concern. He leaned heavily against his silver-filigreed cane, which he'd needed to use ever since a hard voyage to England had nearly killed him two decades before.

"That tooth's far too large to come from a great white shark," her father countered.

"Indeed," Dr. Kelart said. "But the tooth shape is distinct, and unmistakable. If it is not some ancient great white grown to immense size, it is a close cousin."

The imported glass was in fine shape, and Thilini and her father were able to clean all the gears they needed for their submersible prototype. In just a few months, they had his latest invention ready to test in the waters. The gleaming fifteen-foot submarine was skinned in copper and steel, courtesy of the fine craftsmanship of the local metal smiths. The sub was sleek as a dolphin, with round fore and aft windows and triangular fins for stability. Her father's patented, self-contained steam engine powered the screw-shaped propellers at the rear of the sub and electric headlights.

"This is just a miniature version of what I propose to build later," her father remarked to the stevedore, who helped them guide the sub down the wooden ramp into the water. "We must test every aspect of the craft, of course."

"You're letting the girl pilot this thing?" Astonishment was plain on the stevedore's face.

Thilini ignored him and focused on buttoning up her black rubber suit. The feel of the tight material against her legs was strange; she was used to airy saris and sarongs, but skirts of course would drag her down in the water. She hoped the coolness of the sea would help counteract the heat from the steam engine. Otherwise, she'd be stewed like a whiting in a parchment bag before her three hours of air were depleted.

"She knows every rivet and gear of this craft, and she is a far better swimmer than I," her father said. "Further, we had to build the sub at such a limited scale that I can scarcely fit in it myself!"

The men helped her squeeze through the top hatch of the sub.

"Don't go out of the shallows at first, and if the craft is sound, don't take her farther than Pigeon Island," her father admonished.

"I won't," she promised.

They sealed the hatch above her, and moments later the sub lurched as the men pushed it into the water. Thilini said a quick prayer and pulled the lever to start the steam engine. The whole craft shook as the fire ignited in the belly of the sub and the boiler began to steam. She busied herself checking pressure and temperature gauges, then went around the inside of the craft, checking all the brass and copper pipe fittings and wall panels for leaks.

After a half-hour, she was certain the engine was operating as expected and the craft was watertight. She settled in the leather-padded pilot's chair and cautiously steered the craft toward Pigeon Island.

The undersea coral reefs were breathtakingly beautiful; Thilini had seen plenty of brightly-colored fish pulled up by fishermen, but she had never imagined the coral itself would be such a gorgeous wonderland. She felt as though she had been transported to an entirely different world, and that she was not traveling through water but soaring above a dazzling forest on a planet lit by a foreign star.

A pod of curious porpoises swam along next to her craft. Their squeals and clicks echoed through the cabin. The sea mammals seemed to smile at her through the windows, and she could not help but smile back at them as they somersaulted and cavorted.

One porpoise paused and let out a squeal. She and her sisters swam together and huddled with their snouts pointed at each other for a moment; Thilini had the impression they were urgently discussing something. Then they broke away from the sub, swimming fast toward the shallows, all traces of playfulness gone.

What had alarmed them? She peered out through the front window into the deeper water beyond the island. And there swam a lone whale. Not a great blue whale, but a younger toothy orca she guessed was not much longer than the five yards of her submarine. No doubt he was what frightened off her cetacean friends.

I should like to see a whale up close, she thought. She'd seen plenty of dead whales brought to the harbor, but that wasn't nearly the same as seeing one in its natural world. *The engine is fine; a quick look won't hurt anything.*

She pushed the craft forward, gently, to prevent frightening the creature. It was certainly big enough to ram the submarine if it deemed her a threat. The orca turned and gazed at her curiously when she was about a hundred yards away. She stopped the craft, holding her breath, hoping the creature was not territorial.

Suddenly, a huge dark shape torpedoed up from the murky depths below the orca. Thilini saw a jagged maw as wide as her craft open in a flash, sucking the orca down into it, and close with a sickening crack of bone. The force of the bite cut the orca right in two. Blood stained the water in scarlet clouds.

The leviathan shark wolfed the orca down in two gulps, and then righted itself to face the submarine. It looked roughly like the great whites the fishermen had speared in the shallows, but this creature's skin about its head and jaws was armored with thick denticle scales; its snout looked more like a medieval battering ram. And this monster was far, far larger than any sharks she'd ever seen. It was easily four times the length of her submarine.

The monstrous creature began to swim toward her.

Thilini shrieked and pulled the sub around, shoving the steam engine into full speed. She ignored the groaning of the boiler and the rattling of metal as she forced the sub faster and faster, convinced the dire monster was right behind, jaws opening, ready to snap the sub in two.

In her panic, she grounded the sub in the shallows several hundred yards north of the harbor. She killed the engine, got the hatch open with numb, shaking hands, and splashed to land where she collapsed on the sand and gave in to her desire to weep.

After a few minutes, she sat up, dried her eyes as best she could on her sandy rubber sleeves, and walked back to harbor to tell her papa what she'd seen.

Herr Rothschild believed his daughter's story straight away. But since she was merely a girl and deemed subject to frivolous flights of fancy, most others were skeptical and, despite the evidence from the *Southwind*, claimed she'd been frightened by a common cachalot whale or even a mere barracuda.

But in the following week, an East India Company cargo ship was attacked and most of the crew drowned or eaten. And the week after that, they got word of similar disastrous attacks on ships near Colombo and Batticaloa. More and more people heard and believed Thilini's account of the leviathan shark; townsfolk and visiting officials asked her to tell her story so many times that the repetition almost sapped the terror from her memory. Almost. The terrible shark swam through nightmarish seas in her mind when she tried to sleep, and she'd start awake, feeling herself drowning, feeling those awful teeth closing down on her body.

"Our family has lost three ships," Uncle Martin fretted one day. "I cannot take my tea to Europe! The sailors fear this monster like nothing else. We must kill the beast, or drive it away, or else we will be paupers!"

"What would you have me do?" her father asked.

"I would have you build a mighty version of the submersible you tested. Something armed with a powerful harpoon, and a hull built to withstand the pressures of the depths. I would have you build a craft fit to hunt this leviathan down and kill it in its lair."

"If it's a harpoon you need, why not gird a whaling ship in iron and send her and her crew after the shark?"

Uncle Martin shook his head. "The Bombay and British navies have tried that very thing, to no avail. I read survivor's reports; only the head of the shark is visible during its attack, and that part is so well-armored that even harpoons fired from cannons cannot harm it."

"What about a harpoon down its gullet?" her father asked.

"No man who has tried such a shot has lived. The naturalists speculate that the shark may have a softer underbelly that is vulnerable, but there is no way to reach it from the surface of the sea."

"What about explosives?" Thilini asked.

"That, too, has been tried," her uncle replied gravely, "with no better result."

He turned to her father. "We need a working version of your machine."

Her father paused, chewing on a corner of his moustache thoughtfully. "I could build a submarine such as you describe, but I haven't the materials or craftsmen to attempt it."

"I will get you anything you need. Anything at all. I have spoken to officers in the British Navy, and they have agreed to fund your enterprise. Glass, metals, workers ... tell me what you need and I shall get it to you even if I have to strip every estate in Kandy for materials and manpower. We can bring in specialists from Europe by airship."

"All right, then," her father replied. "If it's a fearsome submersible you want, then that's what you shall get."

Thilini and her father put their heads together for several days to figure out what they'd need to build the new craft. Herr Rothschild presented their list to his brother; within days carpenters, welders and masons arrived by balloon to Trincomalee from all around Ceylon to build a fabrication complex at the northern end of the harbor.

Her father hired foremen from a group of engineers his brother recruited, and everyone went to work. Once the construction was underway, it was non-stop. Thilini feared that her father might abandon her now that he had so many educated men at his beck and call, but he kept her close, showing her every engineering novelty his new staff had to show him and every interesting failure.

Further, he introduced her to a brilliant young Serbian engineer named Nikola Tesla, fresh from Edison's laboratory, who helped her solve the problems with their wireless telegraph within a month. She went home to bathe, bolt down quick meals and catch naps away from the noise of the machinery, but otherwise she stayed in the factory and worked and studied and listened and worked some more.

Nine months after Martin Rothschild demanded her construction, the *HMS Makara* was ready. The completed submarine measured 120 feet in length and weighed over 80 tons. The cabin was equipped with compressed air and chemical scrubbers to enable the craft to stay under for up to five days at a time, though they hoped the shark could be found much sooner than that.

Thilini's mother was dead-set against her daughter joining the crew and scolded her husband mightily when she found out about the plan to include the girl as the sub's telegraph operator.

"Isn't it bad enough you let her go out into the water in the first place by herself?" her mother asked.

"She's a brave girl, and she's fine," her father replied.

"Fine? She's not fine! She's barely slept since she saw that monster! I can hear her cry out at night."

"Mama, listen –" Thilini began.

But her mother carried on: "I will not have you take my daughter to her death in that metal casket of yours!"

"We have tested it, over and over. The submarine is as safe as any seagoing vessel."

"She's too young for such things!"

"Too young?" her father replied. "Girls her age are celebrating their weddings; I saw a procession for one girl just this afternoon! How many of them will soon be pregnant, and dying in childbirth next year? Or strangled or beaten by raging drunken husbands who have forgotten their wedding vows? There are so many ways for a girl to die in this world, my dear, and you have seen them all. How many friends did you lose, eh?"

Her mother was silent at that, her eyes downcast. "I lost far too many."

"I do not want to die, and I certainly do not want our child to die," he replied. "But if the worst happens on this venture, her name will be written down alongside mine in the history books. Men years from now will know who she was and what she tried to help us do. And other Tamil girls will hear her tale, and maybe some of them will realize that they, too, could be people of importance in the world."

"Mama," Thilini said. "I *am* afraid of the shark. I see it in my dreams. I don't want it to haunt me when I'm old, but if I do not face it again, I am sure it will be with me forever."

"Oh, my baby." Her mother pulled her in for a tight hug. "Do what you feel you must. But please go to the Koneswaram temple with me first. We must pray to Ganesha to remove all obstacles in the way of your success and safety."

"Yes, Mama."

Four days later, the *HMS Makara* launched with minimal fanfare to go hunting for the ship-killing shark. Her father was the craft's engineer; once they were in the water, he was to focus entirely on making sure the steam engines ran properly. Two British naval men—Hart and Dawes—who were experienced with handling submersibles served as pilot and co-pilot. A third British sailor—Jacoby—manned the triggers for the massive harpoon cannons mounted to the sides of the craft.

Thilini took up her station in front of the gleaming brass wireless telegraph. Her job would be to send back as many details of the hunt as she could. In the event that they failed, at least there would be a thorough accounting of what happened. Technicians had taken one of the wireless telegraphs down the road to Kantale and the transmission back to Trincomalee was a success, so Herr Rothschild was confident it should function well for at least part of the journey.

She took a small mahogany statuette of Ganesha out of the pocket of her rubber suit and set it on the instrument panel. Her mother had given her the figurine after their visit to the temple. Thilini never had much religious fervor, but she felt better knowing the jolly elephant-headed god was there with her.

As her father started the steam engines, Thilini tapped out a test message to the technician manning the telegraph back at the factory; she quickly received her acknowledgement. So far, so good. She began to transcribe the orders the men shared amongst themselves.

"Steady forward," said Hart.

"Aye," replied Dawes. "Ten knots, cabin temperature 80 degrees, boiler temperature 240 degrees."

"All systems fair!" her father called from the rear.

They passed through the area where the orca had been taken by the shark. The crew was silent; all Thilini could hear was the pounding of her own heart. She took Ganesha off the instrument panel and held him tightly in her fist to steady her shaking hand. The porpoises had seemed to be able to find their way in the water not so much by sight as through sound; she wished they had something similar on the submarine so they could better find their way in the dark.

Jacoby the harpooner shifted in his seat a few feet away from her, mumbling a tuneless sea chantey under his breath. His leg jittered, making the metal panel beneath him squeak. His teeth were bad and his breath terrible.

In fact, all the Britons were starting to sweat and stink inside their rubber suits. Thilini decided the best tactic was to breathe shallowly through her mouth.

"Hoy!" Jacoby sat up straight. "I saw something down low off the port bow."

"Taking her around now," said Hart. "Bait the water."

Dawes pulled the lever that released a half barrel of salt pork from a compartment below one of the harpoons.

Thilini watched with growing horror as a dark form rose and rose toward the submarine. When it was 100 yards from the craft, it was clearly the shark and not a whale. Its armored snout was scarred and lumpy from dozens of attacks on ships. It swam closer, attracted by the meat.

Jacoby pulled the trigger on the first harpoon; it struck a glancing blow on the shark's thick gills and tumbled off into the depths. The huge shark veered away and began swimming west. The harpooner swore long and hard.

"I'm after it!" exclaimed Hart. "He'll not escape us!"

"Twenty knots ... twenty five ...." said Dawes.

They followed the shark for hours. The engines were able to keep up with the shark's prolonged speed, but the interior of the submarine became a steampot. Thilini had to fetch a flannel cloth to clean the condensation off the windows every half hour.

Shortly after they lost telegraph contact with Trincomalee, the shark dove down into a valley on the seafloor. Dawes turned on the bright electric headlamps so they could better see. The twin beams cut through the murk, and they illuminated a scene none of them would ever be able to forget.

A huge figure sat there in the middle of the sea floor. At least thirty of the gargantuan sharks circled it; they looked like minnows next to it. At first glance, Thilini thought it was a colossal statue of ten-armed Ganesha. If it sat in the sea beside the cliffs of Swami Malai, she guessed it would be able to peer over the temple built upon those high rocks. But as her eyes better focused, she realized that what she took for elephant ears were really fanning gills, and what she thought was a trunk was a bundle of enormous tentacles hanging down on the figure's distended belly. The arms, yes, those were certainly giant limbs, although inhumanly twisted and ending in too many clawed fingers. And other arms were not arms at all, but massive boneless tentacles.

Surrounding the huge figure for at least two miles around were enormous shards of metal, like pieces of a giant shattered eggshell. They gave off a faint green glow that she instantly recognized.

"The meteor," she breathed. "You were inside it!"

As if it heard her, the hideous colossus turned its gilled, tentacled head toward the submarine and fixed them all in its gaze. Its four eyes were each bigger than their craft, each blacker than the deepest trench in the ocean.

A sudden vertigo took hold of Thilini, and she could feel the terrible darkness of those eyes spreading through her mind, could feel a cold, alien intellect trying to probe the corners of her consciousness. She clutched her Ganesha figure tightly and began to pray.

She could hear her father reciting a Hebrew prayer behind her; there was so much fear in his voice she thought her heart would break. Jacoby had gone slack in his seat, his eyes rolling up into his skull and a trickle of blood running from his left nostril. Hart had fallen to the floor, jerking as though he suffered some kind of seizure. Dawes just sat there staring at the colossus, muttering "No ... no ... no ...." under his breath over and over.

Thilini watched as the colossus casually plucked down one of the circling sharks with a facial tentacle. The shark obediently opened its maw, and the colossus reached inside it with another tentacle, pulling out half a whale carcass. It popped the whale into its tentacle-obscured mouth and ate it as a man would munch a buttered cashew.

The colossus blinked and turned its head ever so slightly toward the sharks. Five of them peeled away from their formation and began swimming toward the submarine.

Thilini swore and leaped over Hart into the pilot seat. She quickly turned the sub around and tried to put as much distance as she could between them and the pursuing leviathans. She glanced at the pressure and temperature gauges. Both were climbing dangerously high.

"Papa! Papa, check the engines!" she cried.

His praying stopped. "What?" he stammered, sounding confused.

"The engines! Attend to the engines!"

"Yes, of course."

She heard him making adjustments and releasing valves, and soon the needles on the gauges were dropping into their safe zones again.

"The sharks!" she called back to her father. "Are they gaining on us?"

"Oh no."

She took that as a 'yes' and pushed the accelerator lever as far as it would go. Forty knots ... forty-five ... fifty. An unhealthy vibration began to spread throughout the sub, the steam engines clearly laboring under the load. She heard her father cursing and twisting handles behind her.

"Dawes! Dawes!" she shouted, trying to rouse the Englishman from his terrified fugue. When her words made no impression, she slapped his cheek.

His eyes popped open. "Ow!"

"I need a navigator, Mr. Dawes. We're headed back to Trincomalee. Can you help me get us there?"

"Aye, Miss." His voice shook and his eyes seemed unfocused. Thilini hoped for the best.

"They're still gaining," her father called. "I have done all I can here to improve the efficiency of the engines."

She thought hard. "Mr. Dawes, do we still have bait aboard?"

"Yes, two barrels worth."

"Dump it. Dump it all. And pray it distracts them," she said, gripping the Ganesha figurine.

He did as she ordered, pushing buttons to release the salt pork into the chilly water.

"Ah!" her father cried, jubilant. "They're stopping! They're stopping!"

Thilini kept the engines hot and pressed the submarine on to land. An hour after they distracted the sharks, she reduced speed and Dawes took over piloting duties so she could send a brief telegraph back to shore.

Martin Rothschild and an array of British naval officers were waiting for them at the harbor when they docked. The morning light was just breaking over the horizon.

"Did we receive your telegraph properly? You said *thirty* of the blasted sharks?" her uncle Martin asked.

She nodded, unbuttoning her rubber jacket to cool off in the morning air. Her cotton undershirt was soaked. "Perhaps even more. And they are but sardines compared to the leviathan who controls them."

Martin looked to her father. "Is this true?"

He nodded gravely, watching medics pull Hart and Jacoby from the submarine; both were completely insensible. "Every word."

"They will eat anything they can devour," she said. "No ship is safe here. No one on Earth has a weapon strong enough to combat the leviathan. I am terrified to imagine the weapon that could, for it would surely endanger all other life on the planet as well."

Martin twisted his gloves in his hands and stared out at the sea. "What shall we do? If we cannot take our tea and timber out on the water –"

"– you can take it by airship," Thilini said. "My father and I thought on this. We have the means to create larger and faster airships suitable for all manner of cargo. Just give us a week or so to draw up new plans, and we may begin building in the factory here."

"What shall we do when that monstrosity has devoured the whole of the ocean?" Dawes was still sheet-pale. "What will we do when it decides to come up on land?"

"Then we will do what we must. But in the meantime, I say give the monster the sea, and we can take the sky."

Her father left to discuss the details with her uncle. Thilini stood on the docks, staring out at the gray expanse of water, remembering the cold touch of the leviathan's mind in hers. She did not know whether it was a solitary conqueror, a lost traveler, or an exile marooned by its own kind on her planet.

But she did know that if it ever emerged from the depths, she would sense it. As she kissed the top of tiny Ganesha's head, she vowed she would move Heaven and Earth to stop it.

About the Author

Lucy A. Snyder is the Bram Stoker Award-winning author of the novels *Spellbent*, *Shotgun Sorceress*, *Switchblade Goddess*, and the collections *Orchid Carousels*, *Sparks and Shadows*, *Chimeric Machines*, and *Installing Linux on a Dead Badger*. Her writing has appeared in *Strange Horizons*, *Weird Tales*, *Hellbound Hearts*, *Doctor Who Short Trips: Destination Prague*, *Chiaroscuro*, *GUD*, *Apex Magazine*, *Nightmare*, *Best Horror of the Year* and *Lady Churchill's Rosebud Wristlet*.

Lucy was born in South Carolina but grew up in San Angelo, Texas. She currently lives in Worthington, Ohio with her husband and occasional co-author Gary A. Braunbeck.

Lucy has a BS in biology and an MA in journalism and is a graduate of the 1995 Clarion Science Fiction & Fantasy Writers' Workshop; her classmates included authors Kelly Link and Nalo Hopkinson.

She has worked as a computer systems specialist, science writer, biology tutor, researcher, software reviewer, radio news editor, and bassoon instructor. In her past life as an editor, she published Dark Planet and selected poetry and software reviews for HMS Beagle. She currently mentors students in Seton Hill University's MFA program in Writing Popular Fiction and coordinates the writing workshops at the annual Context conference.

If genres were wall-building nations, Lucy's stories would be forging passports, jumping fences, swimming rivers and dodging bullets. You can learn more about her at www.lucysnyder.com.

Publication History

"Magdala Amygdala"—***Best Horror of the Year, Vol. 5*, Night Shade Books, 2013.** First published in *Dark Faith: Invocations*, Apex Book Company, October 2012. **Winner of the 2012 Bram Stoker Award for Superior Achievement in Short Fiction.**

"However ...." (co-written with Gary A. Braunbeck)—*Hellbound Hearts*, Pocket Books, September 2009. **Honorable mention, *Best Horror of the Year, Vol. 2***

"Spare The Rod"—*Eulogies II: Tales From The Cellar*, Horror World, July 2013.

"Miz Ruthie Pays Her Respects"—*Dark Faith*, Apex Book Company, May 2010.

"The Cold Gallery"—*Legends of the Mountain State 2*, September 2008.

"Abandonment Option"—*What Fates Impose*, Alliteration Ink, September 2013.

"The Cold Blackness Between"—*Once Upon A Curse*, Dragonwell Publishing, December 2012. Originally appeared in *Aoife's Kiss,* March 2008.

"I Fuck Your Sunshine"—*Vampires Don't Sparkle*, Seventh Star Press, March 2013.

"Carnal Harvest"—*1000 Delights*, December 2001.

"Antumbra"—*Apex Magazine*, February 2014.

"Diamante and Strass"—*Fictionvale,* March 2014.

"Tiger Girls Vs. The Zombies"—*Redneck Zombies From Outer Space*, Woodland Press, 2014.

"Repent, Jessie Shimmer!"—*Appalachian Undead*, Apex Book Company, November 2012.

"The Leviathan of Trincomalee"—*Steampunk World*, Alliteration Ink, 2014.

www.ingramcontent.com/pod-product-compliance
Lightning Source LLC
Chambersburg PA
CBHW030346180626
46812CB00007B/2778